FORGED
BY FIRE

HAZLEWOOD HIGH TRILOGY

FORGED BY FIRE

SHARON M. DRAPER

Thorndike Press • Waterville, Maine

Recommended for Young Adult Readers.

Copyright © 1997 by Sharon M. Draper

Hazelwood High Trilogy 2

Chapter One of *Forged by Fire* first appeared as a short story in *Ebony* Magazine, January 1991, under the title "One Small Torch." It was the first-prize, $5,000 winner in the 1990 Gertrude Williams Johnson Literary Contest.

Published in 2005 by arrangement with
Simon & Schuster Children's Publishing Division.

Thorndike Press® Large Print The Literacy Bridge.

The tree indicium is a trademark of Thorndike Press.

The text of this Large Print edition is unabridged.
Other aspects of the book may vary from the original edition.

Set in 16 pt. Plantin.

Printed in the United States on permanent paper.

Library of Congress Cataloging-in-Publication Data

Draper, Sharon M. (Sharon Mills)
    Forged by fire / by Sharon M. Draper.
       p. cm.
    Companion volume to: Tears of a tiger.
    Summary: Teenage Gerald, who has spent years
  protecting his fragile half-sister from their abusive father,
  faces the prospect of one final confrontation before the
  problem can be solved.
    ISBN 0-7862-7417-4 (lg. print : hc : alk. paper)
    1. Large type books. [1. Child abuse — Fiction.
  2. Stepfamilies — Fiction. 3. Brothers and sisters —
Fiction. 4. African Americans — Fiction. 5. Large type
books.] I. Title.
PZ7.D78325Fo 2005
  [Fic]—dc22   2004030821

This book is dedicated to my sister Vicky, a powerful phoenix rising victorious from the flames and to my friend Marie Randle who fights fires with her fists

ONE

"If you don't sit your stinkin', useless butt back down in that shopping cart, I swear I'll bust your greasy face in!" she screamed at the three-year-old in front of her. He studied her face, decided she was serious, and put his leg back inside the cart. He was standing near the front end of the cart, amidst an assorted pile of cigarette boxes, egg cartons, and pop bottles. He didn't want to sit down anyway because of the soft, uncomfortable load in his pants, which had been there all afternoon and which felt cold and squishy when he moved too much. He rarely had accidents like that, but when he did, Mama sometimes made him keep it in his pants all day to "teach him a lesson."

Gerald was only three, but he had already learned many such lessons. He'd never seen *Sesame Street*, never heard of Riverfront Stadium — he didn't even know he lived in Cincinnati. But he knew the important things — like never mess with Mama when she was in bed — Mama got really mad when you woke her up, especially

7

if she had somebody in bed with her. And never touch the hot thing that Mama used to light her cigarettes, even if the mysterious orange-and-blue fire that comes out of it liked to tease you and dance for only a moment before running away.

Mama had once caught Gerald playing with the lighter, and she made the fire come out and she held his hand right over the flame. It wasn't his friendly fire dancer, though, but a cruel red soldier that made his hand scream and made him dizzy with pain and he could smell something like the meat Mama cooked, but it was his hand. When she stopped, she had washed his hand with cool water and soothed him with warm hugs and wrapped with salve and bandages the place where the fire soldier had stabbed him. She told him that she had done it for his own good and to teach him a lesson. He had tried to tell her that he was just trying to find the fire dancer, but she wasn't listening and he had given up, thankful for the hugs and the silence.

One other lesson that Gerald had learned was *never, never* stay near Mama when she sniffed the white stuff. She got it from a man named Leroy who smelled too sweet and smiled too much. When he leaves, you hide behind the couch and hope Aunt Queen comes over because sometimes Mama yells and gets her belt or her shoe and hits, and hits, and hits. . . . And sometimes she just goes to sleep on the floor and it gets dark and you cry and your tummy feels tight and hurty, but at least there's no shoe to run away from.

Once Aunt Queen had found Gerald curled up behind the couch sucking his thumb. His pajamas were soaked and smelly and he was shivering and hungry. Mama had been gone all day. She had told him not to leave the room, and he had really, really tried to be good, but he was so cold, so very cold. Aunt Queen had taken him to her apartment and given him a warm bath, a bowl of hot soup, and some warm, fuzzy sleepers, even though she had to pin the back of them so they wouldn't fall off. Then Mama had come and she and Aunt Queen had yelled and screamed so much that Gerald had to hold his ears while he lay curled at the foot of the bed. Finally Mama started crying and Aunt Queen was saying stuff like, "I know, honey," and Gerald knew he was going back home.

That night, Mama had hugged him and kissed him and held him close until he fell asleep. Gerald had felt so warm and special and golden — he wanted to feel like that forever. He knew his mama loved him. She had bought him a G.I. Joe man last week and it wasn't even his birthday or Christmas or anything, and most days she combed his hair and dressed him in clean clothes, and told him to say, "Yes, ma'am" to grown folks. And sometimes, on really good days, she would hug him and say, "You know you're my best baby boy, don't you, Gerald? You know you're my baby, don't you?" And he would smile and that warm, golden feeling would start at his toes and fill him all the way up to his smile.

Even though Mama had yelled at him, today was a good day. Mama always yelled — it was no big deal. (Some days he yelled back at her. Then she would slap him and he'd cry and he'd cuss at her and then she would slap him until his head hurt. So mostly he ignored her.) But today was a good day, a shiny day, he thought. The sun was bright gold outside against a clear blue sky. And inside the grocery store there were so many colors and sounds and lights that Gerald just grinned. It was always crowded when they went. Other children would be in carts also and they would have to pass very close to each other. Gerald liked to pretend he was driving a big, fine silver car down the expressway.

Sometimes the cart would be a tank, as he passed cautiously through rows of armed cling peaches and silent sentinels that looked like boxes of Frosted Flakes. And at the checkout lane, the armies rolled smoothly down the long black road that disappeared under the counter. He started to ask Mama where it went, but it was more fun to imagine that it went to a secret hideout where only sweet potatoes and boxes of oatmeal were allowed.

When they got home from the grocery store, Gerald sat on the floor and watched Mama stack the boxes and cans on the shelf. She was whistling — he had never heard her whistle before and he loved the way she laughed as he tried to imitate her. She changed his clothes (and didn't even yell at him for not being a big boy) and gave him two cookies and an apple. Then she went into the other room. When she came out, she had changed her clothes and Gerald thought he had never seen anything so lovely. She had on her sparkly fancy dress that Gerald liked to touch.

"Mama will be right back, baby," she told him. "I just have to go see Mr. Leroy for a minute. You stay right here and wait

11

for me, you hear?" Gerald started to cry, but he didn't want Mama to lose her good mood, so he just nodded and bit his lip. The door closed and he could hear her high heels clicking on the steps. Then it was very, very quiet.

After he finished both his cookies and the apple had turned brown on the white parts, Gerald looked for something to do. It was getting dark and he wanted G.I. Joe to sit with him because the shadows on the wall were getting long and scary. He found G.I. Joe on the floor next to Mama's bed, right next to the cigarette lighter that she had been looking for this morning. Gerald picked it up and for a time he used it as a gun for Joe, then it was a log for Joe to jump over, then it was an enemy for Joe to attack.

Finally Gerald started idly flicking the little red handle. At first it just made a scratchy sound and the smell made him cough and remember how he'd got that brown place in the palm of his hand. Then he remembered the tiny fire dancer, and he wondered if it still lived in there with the fire-sword soldier.

After numerous flicks, he got the fire to stay on. He grinned with delight. The dancer was there, smiling at him and bowing for him, changing from splendid orange to icy green to iridescent purple. The lighter flame flickered magically, making golden the purple shadows on the wall.

With sudden inspiration, Gerald shouted, "Hey Joe, we got a torch!" as he and G.I. Joe marched around the kitchen table. Gerald crawled under the table then, flicking the lighter over and over again to light the way for G.I. Joe. They fought shadows and monsters; they blew up cities and kingdoms. Gerald made the sound effects and G.I. Joe dutifully followed his general into combat. As the mighty battle came to its climax, Gerald crawled up on a chair and stood on the kitchen table, waving his arms triumphantly. *Mama would kill me,* he thought momentarily, *if she saw me up here,* but the thought passed as G.I. Joe fought the terrible mountain man by the light of only a single torch.

Suddenly the tiny light of G.I. Joe's torch was huge and bright as the tip of one curtain in the window touched the flame. Gerald heard a loud *whoosh* and then he turned in terror to see the whole window covered with harsh red flames that crawled and licked and jumped along the window-sill. Gerald scrambled down from the table and ran to his hiding place behind the couch. *Mama said stay here and wait for her,* he told himself. *I know she'll be here in a minute.* He peeked around the corner of the sofa and watched flames consume the boxes of cereal and macaroni that Mama had just bought. When the fire reached the bottle of Big K soda, Gerald watched, fascinated, as the soda bubbled, then fizzed. When it finally burst in a loud, sizzling explosion, Gerald jumped back behind the sofa, coughing and wheezing from the heat and smoke.

He curled up in his usual position then, thumb in his mouth, crying softly. He thought about his mama and how pretty she was. He wondered if G.I. Joe would ever find his way back. And he wondered how he could see so many colors with his eyes closed.

TWO

When Gerald woke up, he didn't know where he was. He was too scared to cry. Everything around him was white — the walls, which seemed to tilt toward him; the sheets, which were scratchy and so bright that he had to close his eyes; and the people, whose pale white faces and uniforms made him think of ghosts that come to get you in the night. His throat felt scratchy and it hurt a little to breathe. And it smelled funny too — kinda like medicine mixed with the stuff that Mama used to clean the floor. Mama — he remembered then. He wondered if she was mad at him. Maybe he was here to be punished. Terrified, he began to cry.

"Hey, little man is coming around! How you feelin', sport?"

Gerald didn't know what to say, or even if he should say anything to this strange white man with the orange-colored hair, so he just stared at him, trying to hold back the tears, needing to go to the bathroom, and wanting to go home.

A pretty black lady walked into the room

15

then, and at first, Gerald thought it was Mama. But Mama never, never wore white, and this lady was smiling and Gerald knew that when Mama came to get him, she'd be screamin' and yellin' and cussin'. Mr. Orangehair walked over to her and said in a voice that was supposed to be too low for Gerald to hear, "Did you get in touch with social services yet?"

"Yes, they're on their way. But that may take all night. You know how it goes."

"Has the mother been found yet?"

"Yeah, she showed up right as they were putting the kid in the ambulance — screaming hysterically about her precious baby. If that teenager from next door hadn't rushed into the apartment when he did, there would have been nothing left of her 'precious baby' but a charred ember."

"You've got that right. Did you get the whole story?"

"From what we can tell, he had been there by himself for several hours, probably playing with matches. A neighbor said the mama was a big-time druggie, left him there alone all the time. She said she usually checked on the boy, but he had been so quiet today, nobody knew he was there. The kid who rescued him told the police that a 'funny feeling' just made him check the apartment before he got out himself. He said he knew the little guy liked to play behind the couch."

"He ought to get a medal. And that mother ought to get . . ."

"Sh-sh-sh. She's already in custody. Child endangerment, abandonment — that sort of thing. Plus, it looks as if he's been abused physically as well — he's got lots of old bruises and scars, and a burned spot on the palm of his hand that doesn't look accidental. Makes me want to scream!"

"Yeah, tell me. You never get used to the bruised or burned or bleeding babies — the kids who've been abused — or the parents who bring 'em in. How old is he?"

"Three."

"Does he have any other relatives?"

"Yes, an aunt, I think. She's on her way."

"Good. Well, I think he's stable now, but I bet he's mighty frightened. See if you can find a big hug for him."

Gerald listened as the pretty lady walked toward the bed. He kept his eyes closed because he was scared and because he didn't want her to know he had been listening. (She didn't know he was an expert in listening to the conversations of grownups — he used to sit so quiet he was almost

17

invisible and listen to Mama and her friends talk about stuff he wasn't supposed to hear.)

"I see Gerald. . . . He's hiding behind his eyes." (How did she know?) Her voice was soft and playful. She took his small hand in hers. "Come on," she said gently, "let me see those pretty brown eyes." Her voice seemed to be smiling, so Gerald slowly opened his eyes. He thought she looked like an angel — with her round brown face and soft white uniform. He wondered if she could fly. He smiled back at her.

"That's better. How do you feel? Would you like some water?" Gerald nodded. She took a spoon and picked out an ice chip and placed it on his tongue. He didn't realize the intensity of the fire in his throat until that soothing ice chip began to cool the flames.

"More," he whispered.

"Sure, babycakes, but let's take it easy." She gently spooned another chip onto his tongue.

"I want my mama," Gerald said, the tears filling his eyes again.

"Your mama's real busy right now, but she'll be here as soon as she can. She loves you very much, you know. But I'm going to stay right here with you till your mama or your auntie gets here, okay? You've been alone long enough. Here's another little chip of ice. Let's see if we can cool that fire."

Gerald relaxed finally, letting himself enjoy the coolness of the sheets and the warmth of her smile. He let her help him to the bathroom, and as she lifted him back into the bed, she hugged him gently. She tucked the soft blanket around him; he sighed and drifted beyond the memories of the day. He slept.

The orange-haired doctor returned, checked the pulse of the sleeping child, and sighed to the nurse. "I wonder what's going to happen to our little friend here. He'll be out in a day or two. But what will become of the rest of his life?"

Just as the nurse was about to answer, Aunt Queen stormed into the room.

Ms. Queen Marie Antionette Lincoln literally filled a room when she entered it. She was dressed in bright red from the top of her elaborate turban to the tips of her polished fingernails, and an air of regal self-assurance seemed to travel with her. Her eyes, which commanded immediate respect, sparked with a fire that matched the shine on her highly polished wheelchair — her throne.

Her voice, loud and authoritative, demanded, "Where is my nephew?"

Doctor Orangehair, probably better known as Dr. McFall, was used to irate or worried relatives, and was not intimidated by Aunt Queen's dramatic entrance.

"If you mean little Gerald, he's just fallen asleep. Let's go out into the hall where we can discuss this without disturbing him."

Without a word, Aunt Queen rolled out of the ward, past the nursing station, and through the large wooden doors into the hall. How she managed to get her chair through those heavy doors just ahead of him so that the door bumped him on the backswing, he wasn't sure, but he thought he saw her smile with satisfaction when he came into the hall rubbing his shoulder.

"I'm Dr. McFall. Your nephew is very lucky. He's suffering from mild smoke inhalation, but he's not burned or otherwise physically injured. Emotionally, the injuries may be much deeper, but only time will tell. He's going to need lots of love and emotional support in the next few months."

"That's why I'm here, Doctor. I've been trying to get that girl to let me take care of the boy ever since he was born. But I gotta give her credit — she tried. She's got a

20

good heart — she really does love him — she just doesn't know much about mothering. She ain't learned how to take care of herself good, let alone take care of a baby. And them drugs ate up what little sense she had. I shoulda stepped in before now, probably shoulda turned her in, but she's family. You understand how it is, don't you?"

"The boy could have died tonight."

"Well, praise the Lord, he didn't. When can I take him home?"

"You'll have to talk to social services and start the paperwork to be Gerald's temporary guardian. Are you his only relative? Does he have a father?"

"Of course he has a father!" Aunt Queen's feathers were ruffled now. "Don't you have a father? I know you doctors are getting pretty good at making test-tube babies, but the last I checked, it still took a mother and a father to make a baby."

"What I meant was —"

"I know what you meant. Since this kid is poor and black and his mother is living alone and unmarried, his father must be long gone. Well, I'm here to tell you that not all black men are like that. There's zillions of black families with a mama and a daddy and two kids like the 'average'

American family." Aunt Queen's shoulders drooped a bit then, and she said with resignation, "But unfortunately, this ain't one of them. I don't know where the boy's daddy is. I just didn't want you to assume. You coulda been wrong, you know?"

Dr. McFall smiled. "You're quite a lady, Ms. Lincoln. How are you going to take care of a three-year-old from a wheelchair?"

"Call me Queen — all my friends do. And like you said, I'm quite a lady. I raised six kids from this here wheelchair. I ain't forgot how. What's one more grandnephew? I'd like to see him now."

"Of course. And, unless there are complications, he should be able to go home by Wednesday."

Aunt Queen quietly entered Gerald's room. She listened for a moment to his slightly raspy breathing, then softly touched his cheek. He coughed, turned, and opened his eyes. At first confused and frightened, he looked around wildly, but when he saw Aunt Queen, he relaxed and smiled.

"Aunt Queen! Where's my mama?"

"Your mama hasn't been feeling well, Gerald, and she's going to a place that's gonna make her feel all better — just like you came here to get better. She told me to tell you that she loves you very, very much. Why don't you come and stay at my house, Gerald, just till your mama comes home. Okay?"

"Can we have oatmeal?"

"Every day!"

"Can I put syrup on my oatmeal? Mama never lets me."

"We won't tell her!" Aunt Queen smiled with a mischievous grin.

"What about G.I. Joe?"

"Who?"

"My G.I. Joe man. Mama got him for me. I left him . . . I left him. . . ."

Suddenly the memories overwhelmed the boy. The flames, the fear, the feeling of utter desolation were too much for him to handle. He cried, huge body-racking sobs. Queen positioned her chair close to his bed, deftly lifted him up, and cuddled him in her ample lap. She rocked and crooned while he wept for all the pain he had known in his short life, and for all the pain yet to come.

THREE

Gerald sat on Aunt Queen's back porch, idly rolling rocks down the wooden ramp that had been built for her wheelchair. In the six years that he had been living with Aunt Queen, this ramp had become his favorite spot. It had launched toy cars and boats, and big-wheel riding toys when he was little; later there had been skateboards and, last year, a go-cart he had made by himself. Of course, he wasn't *supposed* to ride a skateboard or go-cart down the ramp, but who could resist the temptation? Sometimes he liked to lie stretched out on the ramp, his face to the sun, dreaming. Today he was smiling, because tomorrow was his ninth birthday, and he was really, really hoping for a bicycle. It didn't have to be new, just red — and fast.

He was a quiet boy who listened more than he talked and who rarely shared his dreams or fears with anyone, even Aunt Queen, whom he adored. Since the day that she had taken him home when he was released from the hospital, he had lived here with her, under her loving, careful eyes. At first, he had cried for his mother constantly. Aunt Queen had hugged him and hummed old hymns to him and filled in the empty spaces in his heart. Later, he asked for his mother only occasionally, like on his birthday or Christmas. Over time, his demands for her had become weaker, until she had become only a foggy memory.

Life at Aunt Queen's was sometimes hectic, but somehow always comforting and reassuring. Because even though he might wake up and find a stranger sleeping on the sofa, or once, he remembered, in the bathtub (she was real big on showing hospitality to folks in need), he knew that she was always there, and that she would never leave him. Her very presence was like a power source, to be plugged into for love, or security, or a good fried-chicken dinner.

And it wasn't always easy. Gerald remembered times when the lights had been cut off, and the phone, and even the water. He figured getting the water cut off was the worst, because you couldn't flush the toilet. But if it was winter, then doing without the heat and lights was pretty awful. But she managed to get them through it each time, one way or another.

One time, he remembered, she had gone downtown to the gas and electric company because they had cut off the heat. He had been about five, and she had taken him with her. The lady at the desk, who had looked down her nose at them through her funny-looking glasses, had said, "Unless you can come up with a hundred and fifty dollars by five o'clock, there will be no heat."

Aunt Queen had replied quietly, "And unless you come up with some heat by five o'clock, *you* will be on the six o'clock news. I'm poor, not stupid. I know that you can't cut off heat to disabled customers in the middle of winter, especially disabled customers with small children. If you look at my payment record, you will see that I pay on time when I have the money. This month, I just don't have it. Something came up. You'll have your money next month. You have my word on it. You can take my word as my promise, or you can let me take my word down the street to Consumer Alert at Channel Five. I'm sure they'd love to hear how you folks are treating the public, especially after that rate hike you just got."

The heat was back on by four o'clock.

The "something" that had come up was

Christmas. Aunt Queen believed passionately in many things, but Christmas was her supreme passion. She thrived on Christmas carols, delighted in decorations, and indulged in special treats and goodies. The tree went up, with a great deal of traditional fanfare (like making popcorn to string for garlands and making ornaments of soap and old Christmas cards) during the first week in December and stayed up until New Year's Day. The house always smelled delicious this time of the year. One day it would be cookies in the oven when Gerald came home from school, and the next day it would be homemade cranberry sauce. Even in years when there wasn't much money, they managed to have a wonderful Christmas, with Aunt Queen always stretching the cookie dough and the turkey dressing just enough to make ends meet.

His gifts were never frivolous or the result of Saturday morning cartoon advertising, but thoughtful and delightful. Last year, when he was eight, in addition to two books (he loved to read), a new winter coat, and a used but still bright and shiny blue sled, he got a flashlight, two sets of batteries, and permission to explore the basement and the attic (which had previously been off-limits). No amount of money could have purchased the adventures he had in the next few months, exploring the secrets of the outer limits of the house.

In the basement, he had found an old wheelchair, covered with dust and cobwebs. Gerald never thought much about Aunt Queen's being in a wheelchair. Rather than being a limitation, her chair seemed to be merely an extension of her personality. She wheeled around the house and neighborhood with very little difficulty, although buildings without ramps and inaccessible public transportation could really start her to fussing. He knew that she had been born with brittle bones, and that she got fractures easily, and that two of her six children and two of her grandchildren also had the condition. She could walk for short distances, but it was sometimes very painful. However, she treated it the same way she treated any other difficulty in her life — first with a sigh, and then a smile.

"No use stewin' about stuff you can't change," she'd tell Gerald. "It's the things we *do* have control over that I'm worried about. Like whether you're going to finish those carrots — or that book report — before midnight!" He had smiled, and finished both.

She had given him permission to take

the old wheelchair apart, and he had made something that he had called his go-cart. It was lopsided, but it rolled, and when he was in it, he felt like he was king of the world. He had begun it in the basement, but it was cold down there, and there was not much room, so he brought it out to the back porch. Every day after school he hammered and nailed and pounded on it, making it the "ultimate racing machine." (He had heard that on TV somewhere.)

Of course, he had to practice on Aunt Queen's ramp. She had fussed, "You're gonna tear up my ramp, boy. How am I gonna get down it to go to the market if you got it set up like the Indy 500?"

"Aw, Aunt Queen, I ain't messed up your ramp. I made it better! I put racing skids on it, so it won't be slippery for you when it rains."

"Lord help me! Racing skids! Do I look like some kind of race car driver? Next thing I know you'll be tellin' me you put warp speed on my wheelchair!"

But the tar paper that Gerald had found and nailed to the ramp really did help her, so she had let him play on it. He had soon grown tired of the tameness of the ramp, which had a gradual slope, and he looked with interest at the driveway of the house next door, which was steep and sloped right down to the street.

One afternoon, when Aunt Queen was taking a nap, Gerald quietly took the go-cart to that driveway, got on, and rolled cautiously down the big hill. He had used his feet to stop himself every few yards, so it didn't go very fast that first trip. The second time, he only used his feet once or twice, and then it was just to slow himself down when he reached the curb leading into the street. By the fourth or fifth trip, he had increased both his confidence and his speed. He even gave himself a little boost with his feet before he tucked them on the piece of wood that was his rudder, so he sped down the hill this time like one of those bobsledders that he'd seen on TV in the Olympics. Just as he got to the curb, he turned the rudder slightly, rolled to the left, and slowed to a halt by bumping into one of the garbage cans sitting there.

This is awesome! he said to himself. *One more time!*

On that last trip, he had given himself a really big boost to get the most speed possible, and he felt like he was flying. When he had almost reached the bottom of the hill, he turned the rudder to slow himself, but instead of slowing his progress, the rudder came off! Still going full speed, and almost to the street, Gerald could see a long black Cadillac approaching from the left and a dirty green Ford coming from the right. He rolled off the go-cart and into the garbage cans, knocking them over with a terrible commotion. The go-cart sped into the street, where it was first crushed by the Cadillac, then demolished entirely by the Ford, which blared its horn loudly and screeched to a stop.

The driver of the Cadillac never even stopped — he couldn't have known that he had only killed a homemade go-cart, and not a child, but he sped on down the street, never looking back. The driver of the Ford got out of her car, checked to see that Gerald was okay (he had bumped his head on a garbage can), then took him up the steps to the very awake and very angry Aunt Queen.

"Thank you, ma'am," Aunt Queen had said to the woman. "I appreciate your kindness. You saved my boy's life."

"Well, actually a garbage can saved his life, but it could have been tragic. Don't you people watch your children? Letting him play in the street like that! You ought to be ashamed of yourself!" When she saw the blue thunder on Aunt Queen's face, the lady wasn't sure if it was directed toward her or toward the boy, so she backed off a little, saying with a smile, "I'm afraid his little go-cart is a total loss, however."

"So are his privileges — probably for the rest of his life!" Aunt Queen had smiled through clenched teeth as the lady returned to her car.

Gerald had been terrified, because he had never seen Aunt Queen this angry. He was sure he saw blue smoke coming from her ears. She said nothing for at least five minutes. He had to go to the bathroom, but was afraid to move. Finally, she spoke, slowly but explosively.

"You will *never*, as long as you live on God's green earth, do anything that stupid again!"

"Yes, ma'am," Gerald whispered.

"You will *never*, as long as the grass is green and the sky is blue, make me look like a fool in front of strangers!"

"I'm s-s-sorry, Aunt Queen," he stammered. "I was just tryin' to — uh — see — uh — let me explain — I was gonna — but it started goin' — and —"

"SILENCE!" she interrupted. "And you will *never*, as long as you walk the sands of time" — when she got really mad, for some reason she got poetic — "endanger your life again! Do you understand me, boy? Never again! You hear?"

"Yes, ma'am . . . I mean . . . no, ma'am. I mean I promise I won't . . . I mean I promise I understand." Gerald had been so scared and so confused that he wasn't sure which of her demands to answer first.

Then she had sighed and said, "Come here, boy." Gerald had walked slowly to her. "Give me a hug," she'd said finally. "I love you, boy. Don't do that to me again, you hear?"

Grateful and tearful, Gerald had buried his face in her hug.

That had been last summer. The go-cart had never been rebuilt, but the closeness between Gerald and Aunt Queen was probably stronger than ever. She continued to read to him almost every evening, just as she had been doing from the time he had come to live with her, stories of adventure and suspense like *Sherlock Holmes* and *Tom Sawyer*, as well as poetry — Paul Laurence Dunbar and Langston Hughes and many others. Many nights, the rhythm of the poetry had rocked him to sleep.

Gerald was a great help to Aunt Queen around the house — especially in things like reaching and lifting and running errands — and he was even becoming a pretty good cook, learning the basics like hamburgers and scrambled eggs, and even inventing a couple of meals of his own, just to please her.

"Gerald," Aunt Queen would say. "Scramble me some hamburgers."

"One scramburgler, coming right up!" he'd reply with a grin. "It looks a little funny, but it tastes great!"

Now, with only one day to go until his ninth birthday, Gerald was almost as confident in the kitchen as Aunt Queen, and more important, she trusted him to handle any situation there.

He was just about to go into the house to make himself some lunch, and to see if she needed anything from the store around the corner (like maybe cake mix or candles), when Aunt Queen met him at the screen door.

"Sit down, Gerald," she said quietly. "I've got to talk to you."

Gerald tried to remember what he had done wrong. Forgotten to clean out the bathtub? Eaten all the cherry pie? This close to his birthday, he wasn't likely to mess up too badly, he figured. He wasn't sure, but you never can be sure with grown-ups, he thought.

"Did I do something wrong, Aunt Queen?"

"No, child. It's nothing like that. This is something I've been dreading for six years." She paused. "Tomorrow is your birthday, you know."

Gerald started to panic. Maybe she wasn't going to be able to get the bike. Maybe she'd been dreading his turning nine, although he couldn't see why. Nine was cool, as far as he was concerned. What could it be?

"Gerald, you're getting an unexpected present for your birthday tomorrow. . . . Your mother is coming home."

FOUR

Gerald couldn't breathe for a moment. His heart felt tight and crunched inside his chest. All of the hot fears and fiery memories that he had let fade over the last few years were only hidden, not forgotten. He looked up, confused and frightened, and let Aunt Queen soothe him with one of her warm, soft hugs until he was able to speak.

"Mama's comin' here?" he asked quietly. "How come?"

"Well, child, it's like this." Aunt Queen took a deep breath. "It's time you knew the whole story. When I brought you home with me six years ago, after the fire, your mama was tried on child abandonment charges and was sent to jail."

"I knew where she was, Aunt Queen. I just didn't like to think about it, so I let her fade away from me."

"I know, Gerald, and I was never sure if I was doing the right thing by keeping you away from her, but she asked me not to bring you there because she wanted you to grow up strong and secure, and she didn't want you to see her in a place like that. I always sent her pictures of you, and she's kept up with how well you're doing in school and what a fine young man you're growing up to be."

"So when did she get out?"

"She's been out almost a year, Gerald."

He gasped. "A year? But where has she . . . ? Why hasn't she . . . ? I don't understand!"

"She got out, found a job and a place to stay, and decided she wanted to get her life together before she came to see you."

"What about me? It's not fair!" Gerald cried angrily. "She's had a year to plan for all this, and you two dump it on me on my birthday! Suppose I don't want to see her?"

"Then you don't have to," declared Aunt Queen. "But she's been workin' real hard to make up for the past, and she really wants to share your birthday with you."

Gerald just grunted and slumped in a seat by the kitchen table.

Aunt Queen sighed again. "She's got a surprise for you, child."

"I don't think I want no more surprises, Aunt Queen," Gerald answered quietly.

"I understand, child. Tell you what — go out to the garage for me, look under that

37

old green blanket, and bring me what you find. I finally bought me a new sewing machine and I want to try it out."

"Okay," Gerald muttered glumly. He didn't feel like carrying any old sewing machine. He didn't feel like helping Aunt Queen. He just wanted to go someplace and think. He walked slowly to the garage, checked for spiders like he always did, and pulled the old green blanket off . . . not a sewing machine, and not an old, used, repainted bike, but a shiny, new red ten-speed bicycle.

He tried not to grin, but he couldn't help it. He knew Aunt Queen had been saving this for his birthday surprise, and he knew that she had put money aside for months to get such a fine bike. And he knew that she had given it to him today to soften the shock of his mother's return.

As he rolled it out of the garage, Aunt Queen sat on the back porch, smiling at him. "Happy birthday, Gerald," she said simply.

Gerald, whose grin was about to be erased by uncontrollable tears, looked at her, and knew she understood. "I love you, Aunt Queen. It's the greatest!"

"Go on, boy — go try it out. But don't go too far, and stay out of the street, you hear!" She smiled as he took off, waving his hat, T-shirt flapping in the wind.

Gerald rode around the block fourteen times, came in for a glass of Kool-aid, and persuaded Aunt Queen to let him explore a little further. She said he could ride two blocks away, but by the time it was dark, he had explored six blocks in each direction. She knew he needed the time to think and sort things out, so she didn't bother him. By the time he came in at dusk, tired and hungry, he was ready to face whatever tomorrow would bring.

"What does Mama look like, Aunt Queen?" asked Gerald as he was getting ready for bed. "I sorta remember a really pretty lady."

"Your mama always was a pretty little thing," replied Queen. "She ain't changed much."

Gerald started to ask what Mama's surprise was, but he didn't really want to know. Instead he just said, "Thanks again for the bike, Aunt Queen. I promise to be real careful."

"I know you will, child. Now get some sleep."

Queen turned off the light and rolled her chair into the kitchen, where she made herself a cup of tea. She sipped slowly, thinking about the last six years, and how the boy sleeping in the next room had enriched her life with his laughter and energy. Yes, times had been rough for the two of them occasionally, and yes, she was getting older, and yes, her arthritis was sometimes painful, but there was no way she was going to let them take Gerald away from her.

She glanced at the proud new bike on the porch. She was glad she had given it to him a day early. The bike had been in layaway for months, but the joy on his face had been worth the sacrifice. He would need that moment of happiness to hold onto in the next few weeks, for a struggle was coming from which she could no longer shield him.

Aunt Queen gazed at the darkened sky and prayed for strength.

FIVE

Gerald woke the next morning to the sound of voices in the kitchen. He put the pillow over his head, angry that she couldn't even wait until a decent hour to ruin his birthday.

Aunt Queen rolled quietly into his room. "Gerald?"

"Tell her to go away," Gerald mumbled from under the pillow.

"I made pancakes with maple syrup this morning, for your birthday," coaxed Aunt Queen. "Come on and let's have a nice family breakfast, okay?"

"Why'd she have to come *today*, Aunt Queen?" asked Gerald as he peeked from under his pillow.

"She has a birthday present for you — and a couple of other surprises as well," replied Aunt Queen with a tightness in her voice that Gerald had never heard before. "Get some clothes on and be a man. You can't stay in here all day. Besides, I need you out there."

"Okay," sighed Gerald. "I'll be out in a minute — but I'm comin' 'cause of *you*, not for her."

Five minutes later, in clean T-shirt and jeans, Gerald walked slowly to the kitchen. The smell of warm maple syrup would forever be blended in his mind with the events of that birthday morning. For a moment he stood in the doorway of the kitchen, unnoticed.

He thought he had forgotten, but he would have known his mother anywhere. She didn't look much different from the last time he saw her, when her high heels had clicked out of his life and left him alone. She was thin, the color of coffee and cream, with her hair done in fresh finger curls. She wore a red dress — somehow he knew that she'd have on red — that was tightened at the waistline with a shiny gold belt. She was laughing. Unwillingly, he remembered how he used to love her laugh. For a long time it had echoed in his mind like musical memory, and suddenly the song was loud and bright and painful once more.

Standing next to his mother was a tall, chocolate brown man who was looking out of the kitchen window, paying no attention to the nervous conversation or the rich breakfast smells about him. He had hard, muscled shoulders under a tight white T-shirt and crisp blue jeans, and rather than the big brown work shoes worn by most of the men Gerald knew, this man had on shiny black cowboy boots with pointed toes and fancy stitching on the leather. He took a cigarette from the pack in his shirt pocket and had it halfway to his lips when Aunt Queen spoke.

"If you're gonna put fire on the end of that death stick you stuffin' in your mouth, you can do it on the porch. There will be no smoking in my house, young man." He turned, opened his mouth as if to speak, but instead merely gave Aunt Queen a hard look as he put the cigarette back.

Just then, Gerald's mother, Monique, the man with the cowboy boots, and Aunt Queen all seemed to notice Gerald at the same time. Monique inhaled sharply, put her hand to her mouth, and just stared at Gerald with wonder, fear, and admiration. Cowboy Boots had nothing to say, and Aunt Queen decided to let the moment happen by itself.

"Hi," whispered a tiny voice from the largest kitchen chair. It was only then that Gerald noticed the little girl. She was sitting cross-legged in the chair and evidently had been watching him as he observed the scene in the kitchen. Gerald thought she looked like one of those glass dolls that shatter when you drop them. She was the color of pale caramel, with skin thin and waxy stretched over long, delicate bones. She had on a long-sleeved dress that was too big for her and, even though it was hot, long black tights. But it was her eyes that made Gerald stare. They seemed to fill her small face. They were a soft hazel color, and they had seen many tears.

"My baby!" sighed Monique at last. "Can you come speak to your mama, son?"

"Hey, Mama," said Gerald slowly. He didn't know what else to say. So he just stood there, staring at his tennis shoes, wishing that it were yesterday, or even tomorrow.

Monique tried to fill in the blank space between them. "Happy birthday, Gerald," she said, smiling at him. "It's been a long time. But I want you to know that you've always been in my heart. Always."

Gerald nodded uncomfortably. The pale little girl in the kitchen chair giggled.

As if glad to have something to do, Monique picked up the child and, looking at Gerald as if for approval, said, "And this here is Angel, your sister."

"*Sister?*" exclaimed Gerald loudly. "Aunt Queen? What's she talkin' about? I ain't got no sister! And who is this dude with the cowboy boots?"

Aunt Queen, who had been silent, finally said, "Let's all sit down to breakfast and we'll go over the whole story. Jordan, would you say grace?"

Jordan walked his cowboy boots over to the table, sat down, and finally spoke. His voice was rough and gravelly, like he needed to clear his throat. He gave Aunt Queen another of those hard, cold looks, then muttered, "Let Gerald do it."

Aunt Queen, who realized that they didn't need any more tension that morning, replied with quiet authority, "Let us pray. Dear Lord, be with this family. We're gonna need you. Bless this food, and please be with Gerald on this special day. Amen."

Monique smiled nervously and admitted to Gerald, "Well, I guess you've got quite a few questions. Here, have some syrup on those pancakes. I remember how much you like maple syrup."

Gerald just frowned. The pancakes could have been cooked shoes for all he could taste, and the sweet smell of the syrup was making him feel sick. He couldn't understand why Aunt Queen would let him go through this ordeal, especially on his birthday. He glanced across the table at her, and she looked pretty miserable as well. Jordan had a plateful of sausages and pancakes, but he looked angry for some reason. The little girl, Angel, was humming quietly to herself and licking maple syrup from her fingers.

"Gerald," Aunt Queen began gently, "you didn't know it — in fact, nobody did — but your mama was pregnant when she went to jail. The baby, Angel, was born there. I tried to get custody when she was born, but Jordan here says he's her daddy, and he and his mother have been raising her down in Atlanta. This is the first time I've seen her."

Queen smiled at the child, but Angel wouldn't look at her. She just kept pouring maple syrup on her fingers.

"We've been back in Cincinnati for almost a year now, Gerald," continued Monique. "Me and Jordan are married. We got jobs, and Angel is in first grade. I didn't want to come and see you until I could, uh, make you proud of me. So I waited till your birthday." Gerald looked up at her and gave her a half-smile. Monique looked encouraged, took a deep breath, and blurted, "Me and Jordan want you to come and live with us!"

Gerald choked, sputtered, and leaped from the table. "Live with you!" he shouted. "You gotta be kidding!" Tears filled his eyes and he ran out of the kitchen door, letting it slam behind him. He grabbed his bike and pedaled furiously away. It was very quiet in the kitchen for a moment.

Aunt Queen was furious. "Why'd you do a fool thing like that?" she roared. "The boy wasn't ready. You been remembering him every day for the last six years. But he's been forgetting you. I thought we agreed that you'd let me mention the subject to him, gradually, in the next few weeks, after he'd had a chance to visit your place, after he got to know you better and feel comfortable with you. And it was s'posed to be *his* choice!"

"I'm sorry," Monique sobbed. "I couldn't help it! I was just so excited about seein' him. Now I've ruined everything! Jordan, what should I do?" Monique asked plaintively.

Jordan looked at her briefly and shrugged. "Your kid. Your call." He got up suddenly and Monique moved deftly out of his way, but she wasn't quite swift enough. He brushed roughly against her as he was heading out the door. "I'm goin' out for a smoke," he said to no one in particular. He did not acknowledge Aunt Queen, nor did he thank her for the meal.

Aunt Queen sighed. "Gerald will be gone for a while. I'll talk to him when he gets back. We gotta take this slow, Monique. That boy ain't goin' nowhere he don't want to, you understand?"

Monique slumped in her seat and nodded. She completely ignored Angel, who had eaten very little and had not said a word throughout the meal.

Queen said to the child, "Come over here, honey, and let's wash those sticky hands. How about if I slice an apple for you?" Angel nodded. "So," Aunt Queen asked her gently, "tell me what you think of your brother."

Angel smiled softly. "I think he's scared."

"You're right, little one. I think we're all a little scared," replied Aunt Queen.

SIX

Monique and Jordan got tired of waiting for Gerald to return and decided to leave and come back later. Monique was worried, and Jordan, sullen and angry-looking, made her nervous and unable to sit still. They left Angel with Aunt Queen and promised to return in a couple of hours. Angel didn't even look up when they left.

Aunt Queen could see that the child needed some serious mothering. She picked her up with ease, sat Angel on her lap, and just held her for a few minutes. Angel at first was stiff and almost trembling. Gradually she relaxed and let herself sink into the warmth of Aunt Queen's hug.

"So, how do you like Cincinnati, little one?" asked Queen softly.

"It's okay," whispered Angel.

"Do you miss your friends in Atlanta?"

"I didn't have no friends."

"What about your grandma? Don't you miss her?"

"She usta yell a lot. She said she was glad I was leavin'. She said I cry too much."

Queen tensed with anger, but didn't want to show Angel. "It's okay to cry, little one," said Queen as she held the trembling little body. "Nobody's gonna yell at you no more, you hear? Aunt Queen's gonna make it all better. You can cry on Aunt Queen anytime you feel like it, you hear?"

Angel sighed slowly and deeply, then dozed while Aunt Queen rocked her. Gerald walked in then, sweaty and still angry.

"They gone?" he asked.

"Yes, but they'll be back," replied Queen.

"I ain't goin!" he yelled at Queen.

"You don't have to, Gerald. It was not s'posed to happen like it did. She told me that she was gonna ask you if you'd like to come and visit one weekend, to get to know her again, and Jordan, and this little darlin' here. That's all. Ain't nobody gonna take you away from me, you hear?"

"Yeah, I hear you," replied Gerald grudgingly.

"She just got carried away with the excitement of seein' you. She didn't mean no harm." Glancing down at the fragile bit of life in her lap, Aunt Queen asked Gerald, "Tell me, what do you think of our little Angel here?"

"She's awfully pretty," replied Gerald. "But she looks real sad."

"I don't think she's had a very happy life, Gerald. I wish I'd had her with me — with us. We woulda put a smile on that face."

"And some meat on those bones!" Gerald laughed. "She's so little and skinny — she looks like she'll break."

Angel opened her eyes and smiled at him. "Can I see your bike?" she asked. "I ain't never had a bike of my own."

"Me neither," said Gerald, "till Aunt Queen got it for my birthday. Come on, I'll teach you how to ride."

"I can't ride that big old bike," said Angel as she climbed down from Aunt Queen's lap.

"I won't let you fall," said Gerald, laughing as they headed outside.

Queen interrupted them. "Why don't you take off those hot black stockings, honey. It's a real nice day."

Angel looked truly frightened and her large eyes looked like those of a deer, frozen in fear by a hunter's gun. "Oh, no, ma'am! I can't! Mama would get me! Mama would get me!"

"Okay, honey," soothed Aunt Queen. "You can keep them on. I just wanted you to be more comfortable."

Queen looked troubled as they left. That child was terrified of something, she knew. Something was not quite right.

I'm gonna have a good talk with Monique when she gets back, mused Queen. *That baby's missin' some lovin' in her life. And I suspect she's got some hurtin' in her life that I'm gonna put a stop to!*

Queen watched them from the window. Gerald had friends in the neighborhood, but nobody really close. She didn't remember ever having seen him play with a girl. But she smiled as she watched the two children in the backyard.

Gerald, tough, brown, and wiry, seemed almost gentle as he helped the fragile, pale child balance on the bicycle. When the bike got off balance, he caught her and broke her fall, letting the bike hit the dirt rather than Angel. Then he brushed the dirt off her dress and helped her get a speck out of her eye. He was almost — protective of her. Queen thought it was a little unusual, since the two children had just met, but they really seemed to like each other.

Gerald was showing her all of the secrets of his backyard, while she obliged him by being genuinely impressed with his rock collection, his "fighting sticks," and even his treasure box. Her large, expressive eyes looked at him with absolute adoration.

Queen muttered to herself, "Take him away from me? No way! What I need to do is bring that child here with me and Gerald. Poor little thing needs some lovin'."

Suddenly Queen felt flushed and warm. She felt dizzy, then faint. She couldn't breathe. Her arms were tingling. She shook her arms and her head, trying to clear the thickness that was overtaking her. She tried to call out to Gerald, but the pain in her chest made it feel like it was going to explode. She gasped, then fell out of her wheelchair with a soft thud.

SEVEN

Gerald and Angel burst in the door together, laughing. "Hey, Aunt Queen," Gerald began, "can we have some wat—" He stopped suddenly and screamed, "Aunt Queen! Aunt Queen! What happened?"

Queen did not respond. Her eyes were rolled back and she didn't seem to be breathing.

"I gotta call nine-one-one! Angel, run next door and call Mama. Do you know the number?"

Angel, glad to have something to do, nodded, terrified, and left. She could hear Gerald screaming into the telephone.

"Come quick! It's my aunt! She fell out of her wheelchair and she's not breathing! Yes. Yes. The address is 6254 Chambers Street. Please hurry! Oh, please hurry!"

He remembered seeing CPR on television, but no one had ever given him lessons. He tried anyway. He crawled over to Aunt Queen on the floor, tears streaming down his face, and tried to breathe into her tight and silent lips.

"Don't die, Aunt Queen," he moaned. "Please don't die." He could hear the sirens in the distance.

As the ambulance screamed into the driveway, Gerald jumped up to rush the paramedics to Aunt Queen. He almost bumped into Angel, who was coming back into the house.

"Did you call them?" he nearly screamed at her.

"There was nobody home next door. I even tried the next house. I'm sorry, Gerald. Don't be mad at me."

"Sorry. I didn't mean to yell. Come on, the ambulance is here. You can call Mama while they're helpin' Aunt Queen."

The ambulance drivers, dressed in blue, seemed to Gerald to take an awfully long time while they poked and measured and assessed Aunt Queen.

"Is she gonna be all right?" he asked.

"We're doing our best, young man. Did you see her fall?"

"No, we were outside. We came in and she was just layin' there."

"Well, you did the right thing by calling us so quickly. We're going to take her to the hospital now. Is there another adult around?"

Angel spoke up. "My mama's comin'."

Then she looked at the ambulance driver. "I remember you. You tell funny stories."

The driver glanced down at her. "Of course! How ya doin', punkin? No more breaks and bruises?"

Angel looked scared then and ran and hid behind Gerald. The driver looked at him and said, "Take care of her, kid. I gotta go. Your aunt's gonna be at General Hospital."

Gerald looked at Angel with puzzlement. "What was that all about?"

"Oh, he came to my school on safety day," Angel said without looking at him.

Gerald was about to say something else when Monique burst in the door. "I just saw the ambulance leave! What happened?"

"I think Aunt Queen had a heart attack," declared Gerald, who was really starting to feel scared. "She looked really bad. She wasn't breathing," he whispered.

"Well, let's get down to the hospital," said Monique. "Jordan's waiting in the car. He's not real happy, because there's a baseball game on TV and he had to leave before it was over. Hurry!"

Gerald glanced at Angel, but she only looked at the floor. He locked the back door as they left, and somehow he knew that things would never be the same.

Jordan drove them to the hospital, not speaking the whole time. Gerald and Angel sat in the backseat, frightened of him and frightened of what was going to happen. When they got to the hospital, Jordan growled at Monique in his gravelly voice, "Call me when you ready to come home. I can't be sittin' around no hospital all day." With that, he was gone.

Monique asked at the desk, and they were shown to a small waiting room. Gerald didn't like hospitals. He remembered when he had been there before. He felt hot and scared and unable to breathe. Angel kept her head down, wouldn't look at any doctor or nurse who passed by, and refused to speak.

Finally, a tired-looking doctor dressed in blue scrubs walked into the room. "Mrs. Sparks?"

Monique looked up, hopeful, trusting. "Is my aunt gonna be okay?"

"I'm sorry, ma'am. We did all we could. She was gone before she even got here. Please accept my condolences." Monique sobbed.

Gerald, who hoped he had misunderstood, who knew he would die himself without Aunt Queen in his world, said hoarsely, "Is she . . . is she . . . dead?"

"Yes, son," replied the doctor. "I'm so sorry."

Gerald dropped to the floor, buried his head in his hands, and sat there, moaning and rocking, moaning and rocking. The doctor, who knew that grief had to work itself out, patted him on his head and left quietly. Monique looked at Gerald and felt she ought to do something, but she was afraid to touch him or to try to hold him. She was afraid that he would blame her for Aunt Queen's death. So she sat there, wiping her tears with a Kleenex and watching her son shudder with grief in the middle of the waiting room floor.

Angel, who had been watching quietly, walked slowly over to Gerald, sat down next to him, and took his hand in hers. She held his hand, which was cold and trembling, in her small, warm ones. She said nothing. Gradually, his breathing returned to normal and he was able to look at her. He saw pain in her large eyes, and he saw understanding. She helped him up then, and they walked, hand in hand, over to Monique.

Gerald looked at Monique blankly. "Now what?" he asked dully.

Monique, once again trying to fill the

void, but not knowing how, said bluntly, "It looks like this turned out to be a pretty awful birthday for you. I'm really sorry. So I guess you're gonna come and live with us after all. It'll be great. You'll see." She was nervous. "Let's go call Jordan. He'll be so pleased that you'll be living with us." She sounded as if she were trying to convince herself more than Gerald.

Gerald sighed, and with shoulders stooped, followed Monique to the telephone. He didn't care about anything anymore. He and Angel stood there, listening to Monique's side of the conversation.

"Yes, but —

"I'm sorry. . . .

"But we talked about —

"Well, it's not my fault. . . .

"I'm sorry. . . .

"How was I supposed to know —

"But you promised. . . .

"I'm sorry. . . .

"Well, it's too late now. . . .

"I'm sorry. . . .

"It'll be all right, you'll see. . . .

"I'm sorry. . . .

She hung up the phone, turned to the children, and smiled brightly. "He's really happy about it, Gerald. Really, he is."

Gerald just looked at her and sighed.

The only thing that kept him from bolting out of the hospital door and down the street into the darkness of forever was the warm little hand that held his, passing its fragile strength to him.

Angel finally spoke. "I'm sorry about Aunt Queen, Gerald. She gave real good hugs."

Gerald squeezed her hand and smiled a little. "She sure did, Angel — the best in the world. Who's gonna hug us now?"

EIGHT

Gerald was miserable. It was two weeks before Christmas. It had been six months since the funeral, and the loss of Aunt Queen still cut him like a sharp, jagged knife. Life with Monique and Jordan was so different from the relaxed, loving atmosphere of Aunt Queen's house. Monique had tried to make it easy for him, but the small, third-floor apartment was cramped and cold in the winter, cramped and hot in the summer. His precious bicycle that Aunt Queen had given him had been stolen two weeks after he'd moved in. He'd had to transfer to a new school, and he hadn't made many friends. The only person who could make Gerald smile was Angel. She was like a delicate little china doll, special and easily broken. She had a gentle spirit that smiled at him and made him want to protect her from brutes like Jordan.

Jordan Sparks was mean, and Monique was truly afraid of him. He would hit her whenever she made him angry, which was often. She'd apologize and scurry around, trying to please him. When he got drunk, it was worse. One night he had come home drunk and angry.

"ANGEL! ANGEL!" he roared. "Wherezat stupid, skinny kid? Always sneakin' 'round and peepin' from the shadows. Makes me sick. ANGEL! Get in here now!"

Terrified, Angel crept out of bed and peeked around the corner to see what he wanted. Gerald had gone to the store because Monique had forgotten to buy milk and bread. Angel glanced toward Monique's room, but she knew that her mother, as usual, would pretend not to hear.

"You leave that doll on the steps?" he roared.

Wide-eyed and trembling, she nodded slightly.

"Whatchoo tryin' to do? Kill somebody? Get that thing offa them steps and do it NOW!"

Jordan, drunk and unsteady, blocked Angel's way to the door and the steps. She took a deep breath, lowered her head, and scurried past him. But she wasn't quick enough. His fist, like a hammer, connected with her back as she ran. She groaned in pain, but dared not stop.

The steps were dark and narrow and led from the outside door below to their apartment. Angel grabbed the doll and huddled on the steps a moment, tearful and throbbing, trying to figure out how to get past Jordan without getting hit again.

"GET BACK UP HERE! I'M GONNA TEACH YOU A LESSON!" Jordan's angry roaring echoed down the steps. He didn't hear the door open downstairs. Gerald glanced at the trembling Angel, heard Jordan's drunken raging above, and quickly saw what he had to do. He motioned to Angel, left the paper sack of groceries on the bottom step, and quietly tiptoed up the steps.

When he reached Angel, Gerald whispered, "Grab the doll and run upstairs! I'm right behind you!"

Angel looked at Gerald and smiled. She took a deep breath and bolted up the steps toward the waiting Jordan. At the top of the steps, she ducked to the right, just missing Jordan's fist. Gerald leaped into the room, jumped between Angel and Jordan, and the blow came down on him instead. Gerald was tough and strong, but the force of that punch almost made him lose his breath. It would have knocked Angel unconscious.

"Don't you *ever* hit her!" he snarled at Jordan between clenched teeth. Jordan just laughed and hit Gerald again.

Gerald had found out the reason Angel hadn't wanted to take off her long black tights on that warm day last summer. Her legs had been covered with welts and bruises that Jordan had given her, trying, as he put it, to "make her behave." Monique knew about it, but was so afraid of Jordan that she'd accepted it as appropriate discipline. Gerald also suspected that the reason the ambulance driver had remembered Angel was that he had driven her to the hospital for one of those bruisings, although Angel wouldn't talk about it. But since Gerald had arrived, the beatings had almost completely stopped, and Angel loved Gerald all the more for being her protector.

Today, however, the house was quiet. Jordan had stomped his cowboy boots down the steps and down the street. He never said where he was going or when he would return. No one ever asked.

Monique busied herself, trying to clean up the apartment a bit so that Jordan wouldn't have anything to yell about when he returned. She alternated between sweeping the floor and looking out the window for him. Even though Christmas was only two weeks away, Monique had not bothered with a tree or with lights or decorations of any sort for the apartment.

"Are we gonna get a Christmas tree, Gerald?" Angel asked as she walked over to where he was sitting, looking out the window at the cold winter day three stories below.

"I don't know, Angel. Me and Aunt Queen always had a big Christmas. What did you do last year?"

"Not much. Jordan said Christmas was stupid, and Mama agreed."

"Yeah, she probably even apologized for Christmas," said Gerald scornfully. "I tell you what. They've got Christmas trees down at the market where she works. When school gets out tomorrow for Christmas break, I'll stop by there on my way home and see if I can find one for us."

Angel smiled, then inhaled quickly, as if suddenly remembering a bad smell. "Gerald," she said quietly. "Don't be too late tomorrow, okay?"

"Sure, Angel," replied Gerald, not noticing her fear. "I'll find you the best tree ever."

When Angel got home from school the next day, Jordan was sitting in the big chair in the living room, drinking a beer. The shades were down and the television was off. Angel tried to tiptoe past him, but he grabbed her arm. "Where you been?" he snarled.

"I been at school, Jordan," replied Angel with fear and disgust. Jordan's breath really smelled bad.

"Go get me another beer!" he commanded. Angel hurried to get him a beer, hating the fact that she was acting just like Monique, frightened and fearful of Jordan's moods.

"Here, Jordan," said Angel, holding the can out at arm's length. "It's the last one." She was immediately sorry that she had said that, for Jordan grabbed her arm and squeezed, snatching the can from her trembling hand.

Then, instead of yelling at her, or hitting her, he smiled, which to Angel was worse. "C'mere," he said softly. "Come sit on Jordan's lap. I don't spend enough time with my little girl."

"I . . . I . . . gotta do my homework," she stammered.

"Now, don't lie to me, girl. You in first grade — you ain't got no homework — 'specially at Christmas vacation. Now, I said, COME HERE!" He snatched her toward him and sat her roughly on his lap.

Terrified, she could only weep silently as he touched her, rubbing his hand over her arms, her back, her legs. He had done this many times before, ever since she was a baby in Atlanta, but very little since Gerald had come to live with them. "Now, don't that feel good, baby?" he crooned at her. "Just relax. You know you like it."

Angel said nothing. She just wished that he would stop and hoped that he would not want to play "the game." Jordan whispered in her ear, his breath hot and foul, "You remember our secret game, Angel? It's been a long time since we played. You remember the rules. Touching is good. Telling is bad. If you tell, your mama will put you out to live in the snow all alone, and you will die. Now, let's play."

Just then, Gerald opened the door. At first, when he saw Angel on Jordan's lap, he was confused. Jordan rarely showed affection to anyone — not to Monique, and especially not to the children. But to see Angel sitting there, looking so . . . so *uncomfortable*, Gerald thought suddenly. So miserable. Instantly he realized what was happening. Waves of disgust and hot, burning anger enveloped him.

Angel glanced at Gerald. She looked at first relieved, then confused and embarrassed. She leaped from Jordan's lap and ran blindly to her bed. She put the covers over her head and trembled uncontrollably. Jordan, angry that he had been interrupted, slapped Gerald full in the face. "Get out!" he roared. "I'm sick of lookin' at you! You and your mama and your stupid sister all make me sick!"

Gerald said nothing for a moment, but stared at Jordan with hatred and pain. His hands, clenched into tight, angry fists, threatened at any moment to explode with purple rage into Jordan's face. But he didn't want to give Jordan the satisfaction of knowing that he had hurt him, and he didn't want to endanger Angel. Jordan started to hit Gerald again, but the fire in the boy's eyes made him stop. Instead, he grabbed his coat suddenly and ran out.

Gerald went over to where Angel was still trembling beneath the covers and said gently, "Did he hurt you, Angel?"

She peeked out. "Is he gone?"

"Yes, probably to the bar on the corner. He's gone. Did he hurt you?" Gerald repeated.

"No, Gerald, he didn't hurt me, but he scares me so bad. Don't be late like that again, please." Her eyes were dark with fear.

68

"I won't let him hurt you, Angel," swore Gerald. "Guess what?" he said, trying to cheer her up. "I found us a Christmas tree. The man at the market said he'd give it to me. It's just a little one, but it's just right for me and you. Tomorrow, you can come with me to get it."

"What about Jordan?" asked Angel fearfully.

"Don't you worry 'bout Jordan," Gerald told Angel. His voice was tight and tense. "You got me now, you hear?"

Angel relaxed a bit, then took Gerald's strong hands into her small ones. She looked up at him, smiled, and replied softly, "I know you ain't happy here, Gerald. And I know that missin' Aunt Queen makes you feel cold and frozen. I know, 'cause even in Atlanta, I was always cold on the inside — always cold. But since you've been around, I finally feel like sunshine."

Gerald smiled at her, and said gently, "Merry Christmas, Sunshine."

NINE

Gerald awoke on Christmas morning thinking of Aunt Queen. Last year, she had stayed up all night, cooking the turkey, wrapping surprises and hiding them all over the house for Gerald to find. He sighed as he thought of how much his life had changed in just one year. Today, no smells of dressing and sauce and pie drifted to his room — only the strong silent smell of fear and secrets.

Gerald tried not to think about the past or even the future. He survived each day by dealing with necessities — going to school, looking out for Angel, and hating Jordan Sparks. Jordan was mean — he smacked Gerald on the back of his head if he got a C on his report card, he punched him on his arm if he spilled the milk, and he whacked him on his legs for not bringing him a beer fast enough. When Monique tried to speak up, he only laughed and said, "Shut up, woman! I'm gonna make that stupid boy of yours a man!" Gerald had learned to dodge and duck, but he wasn't always fast enough.

70

He couldn't understand why Monique stayed with Jordan. He had asked her once, and her answer was more frightening than the question. It was the Friday before school started. Monique was laughing and dancing to a new song on the radio with Angel. Jordan wasn't home.

Angel looked relaxed and happier than he had seen her in a long time. She was a natural dancer — her petite frame and her long, graceful limbs made her movements seem as if they melted into the music.

Monique collapsed, laughing, onto the couch next to Gerald as the fast song ended and was replaced by a slow, haunting melody. Angel had forgotten their presence, and was moving, eyes closed, to the sweet rhythm of the song. Gerald glanced at Angel, and then at Monique.

"This is the first time I've seen Angel so happy, Monique." (He still couldn't bring himself to call her Mama again.) "She's always so nervous and scared around Jordan."

"Jordan loves that child, Gerald," replied Monique defensively. "Do you know he goes to her room every single night when he gets home just to tuck her in and kiss her good night? Even if she's asleep, he goes in there and spends a few minutes with her. I can't figure out why she acts so scared and stupid all the time when he's around. It gets on my nerves!"

"Aren't you scared of him too, Monique?"

"No, baby, that ain't fear — that's respect. He's a man and I'm a woman. He's stronger and tougher and he takes care of me. It's okay if he gets a little rough sometimes. That's just to show me who's boss, and to show me he loves me."

Gerald, who had grown up with the strength and toughness of Aunt Queen, didn't think that Monique made much sense. He knew he should leave it alone, but he had to ask. "Monique, why don't we just leave Jordan? Me and you and Angel could be real happy — and we wouldn't have to be scared anymore."

Monique, eyes flashing, mood destroyed, turned on Gerald. "You shut up with that kind of talk, you hear! Jordan took you in and buys you food and clothes and tries to be a good father to you and Angel! You better learn some respect, boy! Who you think you are?" She had stormed out of the room then, ripping the radio out of the socket, abruptly stopping Angel's dance.

That was the last time he had tried to talk to Monique about anything more complicated than homework or shoes or mashed potatoes. Angel was right — he felt cold inside. And on this Christmas morning, he felt cold outside as well. He slipped out of bed and shivered as his feet touched the cold floor, then he tiptoed to the window and saw that it had snowed. He smiled in spite of himself. Aunt Queen had loved snow on Christmas morning. The rest of the year she had no patience with it — but Christmas snow was magic snow, she always said.

Gerald wanted to show Angel. It didn't snow much in Atlanta, and she had never seen a fresh Christmas snowfall. He opened his door and was surprised to see Jordan leaving the small room near the kitchen where Angel slept. Jordan didn't see Gerald — he just slipped into the room that he and Monique shared and closed the door quietly.

Gerald, fearful of what he might find, refusing to even imagine what he had discovered, raced across the cold floor and opened Angel's door. Her bed was empty. Huddled in a corner, shivering in her thin nightgown, clinging to an old doll's blanket, Angel was crying silently.

She looked up in fear when Gerald entered, and backed farther into the corner.

"No!" she whispered. When she saw it was Gerald, she cried even harder.

"It's freezing in here, Angel," said Gerald gently as he pulled the blanket off the bed and put it around her. He didn't ask her any questions. He handed her a sweatshirt and a pair of jeans, and some socks from the box where Monique kept Angel's clothes. She dressed quietly and quickly and followed him to the front room where the small, thin tree stood decorated on the coffee table. With the blanket wrapped around both of them, they sat on the sofa in the darkness of that Christmas morning, silent and sorrowful.

Finally Gerald spoke. "It snowed last night. Come look."

Angel looked with wonder at the sparkling snow. "Everything looks so *clean!* It's like all the bad stuff is covered up with shiny stuff," she said, barely smiling.

"Aunt Queen used to say that Christmas snow was magic snow," Gerald told her. "Make a wish, Angel."

Angel squeezed her eyes tightly, held her breath, and whispered softly, "Please! Please! Please! Please! Please!"

"Angel," Gerald said, gently interrupting her, "we gotta get help. We gotta tell somebody. We can't let him bother you anymore!"

"No!" she almost screamed. "He'll hurt Mama. He'll hurt you. He'll hurt me bad! He told me and I believe him. It's not so bad. He just . . . he just . . . talks to me."

"I'm gonna tell, Angel," Gerald insisted. "I gotta tell somebody."

"Please don't, Gerald. If you do, I'll run away and hide in the snow. I'll say you're bad and you made it up!" Angel was almost hysterical.

"Okay, okay! Calm down. I won't say anything now, but I want you to sleep in my room. You can sleep in the other twin bed. We'll tell Monique that you're scared of the dark."

"She won't care," replied Angel, "but Jordan will be real mad."

"I have an idea!" said Gerald suddenly. "But we have to work fast."

Gerald ran to the area under the sink where Jordan kept his tools. He grabbed a screwdriver and a wrench and ran to Angel's room. Swiftly he wriggled under the bed. Mystified, Angel heard the sound of the tools on the metal frame of the small bed. Gerald emerged, grinning. In his hand were six screws and two bolts. He tossed them into his pocket and hurriedly replaced Jordan's tools just as Monique and Jordan emerged from their bedroom.

"I'll tell you later," he whispered to Angel with a grin.

Monique smiled sleepily and said, "Merry Christmas, my babies. Did you see the snow?"

Angel gave Gerald one quick look. It was a pleading one. He sighed and shook his head just a bit to show her he would not tell — at least not yet, he thought. Angel smiled sweetly at Monique. "Merry Christmas, Mama! It's magic snow. Gerald told me so."

Gerald glanced at Jordan, who seemed to be relaxed and enjoying the snow. Jordan looked at Angel and, in that gravelly voice that Gerald hated, said to her, "I got you a Christmas present, Angel."

Angel looked surprised. Jordan had never bought her anything special, not even on her birthday. Monique scurried back into the bedroom, brought out the box that the last pair of Jordan's new shoes had come in and handed it to Angel with a grin. "Here, baby. Open it. Quick!"

Gerald could hear scratching coming from within the box. Angel opened it, and out popped a tiny ball of tawny fur, which landed in her lap. "A kitten!" screamed Angel with delight. "I'm going to name her Tiger!"

Gerald was glad to see Angel smiling again. But he knew that this happiness would not last. He glanced at Jordan and Monique. Monique was watching the snow. Jordan was watching Angel.

TEN

When Jordan found out that Angel's bed was broken, he was angry and tried to fix it. But Jordan had no skill at fixing and repairing and he quickly gave up the task with a curse and a kick to the bed. He then tried to move Gerald's extra bed to Angel's room, but it wouldn't fit in the small corner room where she slept, so he gave up, swearing he would buy a new bed as soon as he got a little cash. Gerald and Angel giggled at Jordan behind his back, and Angel moved to the other twin bed in Gerald's room.

Angel was happy with Tiger the kitten and the safe sleeping arrangements. Gerald would read to her late at night, trying to remember the poems and stories that Aunt Queen had read to him. Sometimes they would hear Jordan coming in late from his job. His boots were always loud on the bare floor, but he never came into the room.

He still smacked Gerald around whenever he got the chance, but not as frequently as he used to. He had a new job which he liked, and was getting paid every week. Monique was like a little butterfly. She fluttered around the house, trying to make sure Jordan was happy. Gerald wondered when Monique ever got a chance to be happy herself, or if she even thought about it. But he never asked.

She couldn't cook very well, so they ate a lot of fast food. Gerald missed Aunt Queen's home-cooked meals. He missed her home-cooked loving even more.

Tiger loved french fries. She would jump up on the table and eat them right out of the bag. However, she knew to stay away from Jordan, who would knock her off the table with a sweep of his arm, or kick her if she got in his way. Angel would grab the cat and hug her until she stopped shaking and began to purr again. She dressed the cat up in doll clothes, pulled her along the floor in a box, and even decorated her tail with ribbons. Tiger allowed it all without complaint, snuggling each night at the foot of Angel's bed.

When Angel got chicken pox, Tiger seemed to be pleased to have Angel home from school each day. Monique took two days off from work, mostly to watch the soaps, but she did open a can of chicken soup each day and give it to Angel. Angel hated chicken soup, so Tiger had great lunches.

On the third day, Monique had to go back to work. Gerald had already left for school. Angel was still asleep.

"I'll watch her," Jordan growled carelessly.

"What about your job?" Monique inquired hesitantly.

"Don't you worry about my job, woman! You just do yours! I said I'd watch the kid and that's what I'm gonna do! Now get to work!" Monique hurried out the door.

"She loves chicken soup!" she called to Jordan as she left.

When Angel woke up, she felt for the warm lump in the blanket called Tiger. The cat was gone. Angel felt itchy, but not as sick as at first. She hoped Mama had fixed peanut butter today. She was sick of soup.

Angel got up, went to the bathroom, and tried not to scratch her spots. "Tiger?" she called. *Where could she be hiding?* Angel thought.

Still concentrating on finding the cat, Angel didn't see Jordan until it was too late. He was sitting on her bed. She gasped and tried to run from the room, but he grabbed her arm and pulled her fiercely next to him.

"No, please, no, Jordan," she begged. "Please don't. Oh, please don't."

"Relax, girl. I ain't gonna hurt you. I just want to talk to you, to see how you feel."

"I feel fine, Jordan. Now leave me alone! Please!"

"Now you just let me *see* how well you feel. How's that rash? Hold up your shirt and let me see."

"No, Jordan! I don't want you to look at my rash. No!"

"I'm your daddy, girl. I'll look at your rash if I want to! How can I tell if you're getting better? Now take off that shirt!" Angel tearfully removed her T-shirt while Jordan watched. Her rash was very mild and the spots were already beginning to fade. He touched her back, and she tensed at the roughness of his fingers.

Angel wept silently while he explored her body for chicken pox spots. He took his time. He found them all.

Finally he spoke. "I've missed you, girl. I forgot what a special little Angel you really are." He headed out of the room.

"Oh, by the way, if you're lookin' for that stinkin' cat, it's in the oven. Don't worry, I didn't turn it on. But if you say one word to anybody — I swear I'll kill that cat and cook it!" With that, he slammed the door of the apartment and left.

Angel was alone. Still shaking and sobbing, she ran to the kitchen and slowly opened the oven door. Tiger jumped into her arms. They stood there for a minute, clinging to each other in fear of the darkness they had seen. Angel, too terrified to tell and too frightened not to, clung to her cat and wept.

ELEVEN

When Gerald got home, Angel was pale and feverish. Jordan had not come back all day. Gerald fixed Angel a scrambled egg and gave her some juice. She would not talk to him. He remembered when he got chicken pox how Aunt Queen had made a warm poultice out of something she found in the garden, and the itch had disappeared. What was bothering Angel seemed to be more than a rash. Gerald carried the worry deep and heavy in his gut.

"Monique," he called to her as soon as she walked in. "I think Angel's getting worse. Come look."

Monique sighed, glanced at Angel, and replied, "These things take time, Gerald. If she ain't better by tomorrow, I'll take her to the clinic. Right now I'm going to give her something for her fever and a little of my good chicken soup. Let's see if that helps, okay?"

"Why did you leave her here by herself?" Gerald asked. "I coulda stayed home from school."

"There was no need for you to stay home. Jordan stayed with her today."

At the sound of Jordan's name, Angel's eyes got wide, but she said nothing. She moaned softly, then was silent again. Gerald frowned.

"Well, he wasn't here when I got home from school," Gerald replied. "She's too little to be here all by herself."

"Maybe he went to get some french fries for Tiger. You know he likes that cat," suggested Monique as she checked her hair in the mirror.

Tiger was curled into a tight ball, very close to Angel. "Let's let 'em sleep, Gerald," said Monique. "I bet they'll both feel better in the morning."

Gerald didn't sleep well. He watched Angel toss and turn and moan. He was worried.

Finally, just before dawn, he gently shook her arm.

"Angel!" he said quietly. "Angel!"

She woke suddenly, eyes fearful and staring. Instinctively she grabbed the covers and pulled them tightly around her.

"It's me, Gerald. How do you feel?"

Angel relaxed a bit and turned away from him.

"I'm okay, Gerald. It's just chicken pox.

Let me get some sleep."

"What about Jordan?"

"He ain't got chicken pox."

"I gotta know, Angel. You gotta tell me. Did he bother you yesterday? Did he hurt you?"

"I'm cold, Gerald."

He pulled an extra blanket out of the closet and tucked it around her.

"I'm always cold, Gerald, and scared. Jordan makes me feel like I'm cold and dead inside. He . . . he said he would kill Tiger. He said he would kill Mama. Make him go away, Gerald. Make him go away."

"Did he touch you, Angel?" Gerald asked. He felt the anger rise like vomit in his throat.

"I'm so cold." Angel refused to look at Gerald. She stared into the darkness, shivering with her fear.

"Go back to sleep, Angel," Gerald said, trying to soothe her. "I'm gonna make things better. Do you trust me?"

"Yes," she whispered softly.

"I'll be back as soon as I can."

"Don't leave me here with Jordan!" Angel whispered frantically. "Where's my cat?"

"Tiger's right here at the foot of your bed, and Monique doesn't have to go to work until later. You'll be fine until I get back. Go back to sleep and relax. I'm gonna take care of you, okay?"

"Okay, Gerald," she replied with sleepy trust. She sighed and drifted back to sleep.

Gerald dressed quickly, took his book bag, and left the apartment. It was 6 a.m.

Monique got up about seven and decided to go to work early to put in some overtime. She noticed that Gerald was already gone. She shrugged, assumed he had gone to school early, and finished polishing her nails. She glanced at Angel, who was still asleep, but she didn't wake her; nor did she touch her to see if the child was feverish. She decided to change her shoes because they didn't match her dress, and left to catch her bus.

Gerald felt sick. He knew he had to get help in a hurry, but he didn't know where to go, who to talk to, or what he should do first. The bus dropped him off in front of Hazelwood Middle School, where he was in sixth grade. It stood empty and silent this early in the morning. The dark upstairs windows looked like huge, accusing eyes, staring at him. The front door hadn't even been unlocked yet. Gerald sighed and sat on the curb, hoping that a teacher or counselor he knew and could trust would decide to come to work early today.

He was hesitant to go to the police.

What if they don't believe me? he asked himself. *Will they believe a kid? I don't really have any proof. On TV, cops need hard evidence or the bad guy gets away. What if I accuse Jordan of abuse or something and they can't prove it? He'll be angry and get even more violent and maybe hurt Angel and . . .*

Gerald bowed his head and sighed in misery. He barely noticed the silver Buick that stopped in front of him.

"What's up, man? You look so down that curb looks like up." It was Robbie, the best basketball player at Hazelwood Middle School. Gerald liked Rob, who was always cracking jokes and acting silly.

"What you doin' here so early?" Gerald asked.

"My dad drops me off every morning before he goes to work. It's a little early, but I finish up my homework or go sleep in the locker room. That door is always open early. Want a doughnut?"

"Naw, man. I got a lot on my mind today."

Rob's dad, who was standing at the back of the car getting Robbie's bag and lunch out of the trunk, glanced at Gerald with concern.

Gerald didn't know Rob's dad very well, but he probably knew him better than any father of his friends. Mr. Washington was active on the school parent council and came to all of the basketball games, track meets, and school plays. He and his wife often had Rob's friends to their home on weekends. They had a finished rec room, a huge backyard, and a refrigerator that always seemed to be well-stocked with essentials like pizza and ice cream and soda pop. Gerald wasn't sure if they were wealthy or not, but they sure had lots of things that he and Monique and Angel couldn't afford. Gerald had only been there once, and although he'd felt uncomfortable at first, Rob's family had made him feel at home.

Mr. Washington touched Gerald on the shoulder. "You all right, son?" he asked with genuine concern.

Gerald had planned to shrug, laugh, and head to the gym with Rob. But the touch of Rob's father's hand on his shoulder seemed to let everything come loose. He tried to hold them back, but tears of fear and worry began to escape from his tightly clenched eyes.

Embarrassed, he sniffed and lowered his head. Rob's father motioned for his son to go on into the building and squatted on the curb next to Gerald.

"Let's go get something to eat, Gerald," he said quietly. He offered his hand. Gerald sighed, wiped his eyes on his coat sleeve, took the offered hand, and got in the car.

Mr. Washington asked no questions at first. At McDonald's he ordered a cup of coffee and a hot chocolate, got extra cream and sugar for both, and steered Gerald to a booth near the back. Gerald sipped the cocoa gratefully, the warmth of it relaxing him. He thought of Aunt Queen, who loved her black coffee every morning. He knew that Queen would have liked Rob's dad. She approved of black men in blue suits who had jobs in offices downtown. Mr. Washington had called his office from a pay phone, so he casually read the morning paper while Gerald sat silently, trying to figure out where to start.

"It's my sister," he said finally.

"How old is she?"

"Almost seven. Her name is Angel."

"Is she sick?"

"No, she, uh, well, she's got, uh, chicken pox."

"I thought you said she wasn't sick."

"Well, the chicken pox is not the

problem. See, she can't go to school, so Jordan stays with her and he, and he . . ."

"Who's Jordan?"

"My stepfather. He drinks, and he's mean, and he smacks me around, but that's not the problem — I can handle it. I think he's . . . doing stuff to Angel that he shouldn't. And I don't know what to do! I can't go to the cops — they might not believe me. She's so scared of him she won't even admit it to me, but I know he's hurting her and I don't know what to do or who to tell or . . ."

He stopped, in tears again, but this time, he wasn't ashamed. He felt cleaner now that he had finally told someone. Someone who he knew could help.

"You were right to tell me, Gerald," Mr. Washington assured him with a sigh. "I'm glad you trusted me. Let's go get this stopped right now. Where is this Jordan?"

"At home. With Angel."

"Let's hurry. We're going to the police."

TWELVE

Jordan took out a cigarette, put his feet up on the coffee table, and smiled, looking forward to another day with his little Angel.

When Angel woke up, the cat was missing again, and she could hear Jordan's boots as he walked around the apartment. He was whistling.

She looked at the window. It was narrow and had been painted shut years ago. Even if she hid under the bed, there was no escape. She felt like she was going to throw up. Jordan's footsteps approached. He opened the door. He was smiling.

"I brought breakfast in bed for my little girl," he said cheerfully. "Come and eat. You look a little pale."

Angel darted past him out of the bedroom door and mumbled, "I have to go to the bathroom." She stayed in the bathroom as long as she could, but the door had no lock, and she watched as he turned the knob from the outside.

"Your breakfast is getting cold," Jordan declared. "Don't you appreciate what I've done for you?"

"Thank you, Jordan, for the breakfast, but I'm not very hungry. Where's my cat?"

Jordan's loud laughter startled her. "Ha! You think I killed that stupid cat? Not yet. Maybe I won't have to. Come here!"

Angel's feet would not walk toward Jordan. His boots clumped on the bare wood floor as he walked over to her. He picked her up, then kicked open the bedroom door. He placed her gently on the bed. "Today," he said softly, "we got the whole day to spend together. Ain't that grand?"

Angel trembled with disgust and fear. Jordan turned the radio up loud and closed her door.

Jordan didn't hear the apartment door open. He didn't notice that Gerald had quietly opened Angel's door or that two uniformed police officers were standing there until just before they grabbed him and handcuffed him. He roared in anger and tried to get away, but it was too late.

"Jordan Sparks — you are under arrest. You have the right to remain silent. Anything you say or do can and will be used in a court of law. You have the right to . . ." They dragged him, screaming and cursing, from the house. Gerald watched with a grim smile.

"What happened, Gerald? How did you know? He said he'd kill Tiger! I'm sorry, Gerald! It's all my fault!" Angel was almost hysterical. Relieved at escaping what she feared and dared not imagine, she did not know how to react.

Gerald tried to calm her down. "Sh-sh-sh," he whispered. "I found someone that we could trust. I told him everything. He called the police and helped me to convince them to come here right away. I was afraid I would be too late."

"Oh, Gerald, was I bad? Is Jordan going to get in trouble because of me? It's all my fault!"

"No, Angel," soothed Gerald. "It's not your fault. Not even a little bit. Jordan was a very bad man. He was doing bad things. You did the right thing. I'm going to be here for you and everything is going to be better — I promise."

Angel cried then, not for Jordan, but for herself and for lost dreams and for secrets in the night. Finally she stopped sobbing and looked up at Gerald, who had wrapped his arms protectively around her. "Where's my cat?" she asked.

Gerald laughed and let Tiger out of Monique and Jordan's bedroom. Angel squeezed the cat so hard that she burped!

Gerald and Angel began to laugh uncontrollably. Gerald almost wet his pants and Angel fell on the floor, rolling in laughter. That's how Monique found them when she marched through the door, angry and upset.

"What's so funny?" she screamed. "You think it's funny to send a man to jail for something he ain't done? You lowlife children! I ought to kill both of you! How dare you lie on a good man like Jordan?"

Instantly serious, Angel and Gerald looked at Monique in amazement. "Mama, it's true. I didn't make it up. Jordan's been . . . uh . . . been bothering me for a long time. He comes in my room at night and he —"

"You lie!" roared Monique. "You filthy liar!"

Gerald spoke up. "I saw him do it, Monique. She ain't lying. He told her he would kill her cat if she told. I was the one that told. I've seen him coming out of her room at night. I'm sorry, Monique, but it's true."

Monique threw her purse at him and burst into tears. She ran into her bedroom screaming and sobbing. Gerald and Angel exchanged glances. "Looks like it's me and you, kid," Gerald said quietly. "Just me and you."

THIRTEEN

Gerald and Angel couldn't have made it through the trial without Mr. Washington. Monique was sometimes angry, often irritable, and always tense. She yelled at Angel for spilling her milk and blamed Gerald for the toast that she had burned. At the trial, she insisted on wearing a bright red satin dress even though Gerald and Angel told her to wear something a little more business-looking.

"If that's the last Jordan's gonna see of me before you two lyin' devils send him away, he's gonna remember me as lookin' good!" she exclaimed.

"We ain't lying, Mama," Angel tried to explain, but Monique refused to listen — she didn't want to hear it.

On the first day of the court proceedings, Gerald held Angel's hand as they sat on the worn brown wooden bench in the hall outside the courtroom. Monique's high heels clicked on the polished floor as she paced back and forth. She went down the hall to the bathroom six times in half an hour to check her makeup and hair. No one spoke. Just as the bailiff came into the hall to call them to the courtroom, Mr. Washington turned the corner and strode toward them, smiling.

Gerald looked up and grinned with pleasure and relief. "I didn't expect — I mean — I'm surprised — I mean — man, am I glad you're here!"

Mr. Washington replied in his deep, cheerful voice, "I figured you might need another hand to hold. Hi there, Angel."

Angel looked up shyly, but did not speak. Monique, returning from still another makeup check, patted her hair and smoothed her dress as she approached the tall, well-dressed man speaking to Gerald.

"Monique, this is Darryl Washington. He's —"

Just then, the court clerk called them a second time. Gerald was relieved that he didn't have to explain to Monique exactly how Mr. Washington had helped them. Not only had he helped Gerald and Angel file the proper papers to explain to the courts exactly how Jordan had been molesting Angel, but he had also made sure a caring and understanding social worker was assigned to their case, and he had found a wonderful female counselor for

Angel — someone she could talk to about the bad dreams she sometimes had, and the bad feelings left over from her experiences with Jordan.

Monique gave one more curious glance at Darryl Washington as she hurried in to the courtroom. She left the children standing in the hall, unsure of what to do. Mr. Washington took their hands, squeezed them in assurance, and escorted them into the courtroom.

Jordan sat at a table on the right side of the room, his face angry, glaring as Angel and Gerald walked into the room. Jordan's lawyer, a thin man with dirty fingernails, shuffled his papers and checked his watch frequently. Monique sat in the first row, across from Jordan, in a position where he could see her well. She smiled at him, but he didn't even look at her.

On the right side of the room sat the jury. Mostly women, they looked at Angel and Gerald without smiling, but their eyes showed understanding and perhaps even a bit of sympathy. Gerald and Angel were told by the prosecutor that they would only have to answer a few questions and then they could leave the room. She told them that neither one of them was in trouble, and not to be overwhelmed or frightened by the proceedings. It was Jordan, she reminded them, that had done wrong, and he was the only one on trial. They were just witnesses. Gerald relaxed a bit and breathed in slowly. He felt stiff and uncomfortable in the tight dark suit and afraid of all the strangers who seemed to be controlling his life today.

Angel trembled and sat close to Gerald. Mr. Washington sat in the row behind them and patted their shoulders. "I'll be right here, kids. Just relax and tell the truth. You'll be fine."

Gerald nodded, but he felt sick and dizzy. Angel's eyes were closed and she breathed slowly and carefully. The prosecutor, a round woman dressed all in green, including green fingernails done to match her bright green shoes, began by explaining to the jury what the charges were against Jordan, describing him as "a despicable monster." She said she hated putting the children through this, but their testimony was essential. Gerald's name was called first.

"State your name, son."

"Gerald Nickelby."

"Do you understand that everything you say here must be the truth?"

"Yes, ma'am."

"What grade are you in?"

"I'm in the sixth grade at Hazelwood Middle School."

"How long have you been living with Jordan and Monique Sparks?"

"Two years — ever since my aunt Queen died."

"Do you get along with your parents?"

"Monique is my mother, but Jordan is *not* my daddy. He's Monique's husband, and he says he's Angel's daddy, but he's no father of mine!"

"What kind of father is Jordan?"

"No kind! He smacks me and punches me all the time. I got cuts and bruises all over me. But that ain't the problem. I can deal with that. It's what he does to Angel that I can't stand."

"Can you explain?"

Gerald looked at Monique. She was looking at Jordan, whispering "I'm sorry" across the room. Gerald looked away in disgust and glanced at Mr. Washington. He still couldn't believe that a busy man would take the time to come and be with them. Mr. Washington smiled at Gerald in encouragement.

Gerald took a deep breath. "He goes into Angel's bedroom at night. He's messin' with her and it makes me sick!"

"Have you ever seen him touch her in an improper way?"

"Well, no, but I know he does."

"Did she ever tell you?"

"She was really scared, but yeah, she told me about it finally. So I got help and the police found him in her bedroom."

"Thank you, Gerald."

The defense lawyer asked only a few questions. "Gerald," he began, "Mr. Sparks says you are lying. If you have never really seen him doing anything to Angel, how can you sit there and accuse him with no proof?"

"I see how scared Angel is and I see how Jordan likes to touch her hair and put his hands on her back. I am *not* lying!"

The lawyer shrugged, checked his watch, picked his nose, then said carelessly, "No further questions." Gerald sat down gratefully.

When Angel's name was called, she almost fainted. Gerald walked with her and helped her sit in the witness chair.

"I'm only going to ask you a few questions, honey, okay? Don't be afraid. Just tell the truth."

Angel nodded, barely able to breathe.

"Tell us your name."

"Angel Sparks."

"Do you understand that everything you say here must be the truth?"

"Yes, ma'am."

"What grade are you in?"

"Second grade."

"We're going to use this doll, okay? You just point to the doll to help you answer the questions, all right?"

Angel nodded again, and hugged the doll the prosecutor gave her.

She asked her about Jordan and what life was like with him. Angel whispered her answers, but she told the truth.

"Are you afraid of him?"

"Yes, ma'am."

"Can you tell us why?"

"He yells."

"Is that all?"

"He hits."

"Does he hit you?"

"Sometimes. Mostly he hits Gerald and Mama."

"Does he ever hurt you?"

"Sometimes."

"How?"

Angel hesitated. "He makes me play games."

"What kind of games?"

"Bad games."

"Can you explain what kind of bad

games? I know this is hard for you, but we're almost finished."

"Touchy-feely games."

"Can you show me on the doll?"

The doll was really helpful. When the prosecutor asked Angel where Jordan had hit Gerald, for example, Angel pointed to the doll's back and face. And when she was asked about where Jordan had touched her, Angel was able to use the doll to show what he had done.

When the prosecutor was finished, the defense lawyer whispered to Jordan, started to get up, then sat back down. "No questions, Your Honor."

"Thank you, Angel," the prosecutor in green said. "That's all. You and Gerald can leave now. You were very brave."

Angel and Gerald walked out of the courtroom together. Neither looked at Jordan. Monique refused to look at them. Mr. Washington took them both to lunch, but Angel couldn't eat.

It took the jury less than an hour to decide his fate that afternoon. He was found guilty on all counts, and the judge, sentencing him immediately, gave him six to ten years in prison. As he was taken away, Angel finally breathed deeply. Gerald watched the door close and smiled with grim satisfaction.

Finally, Jordan would be in a place where he could no longer threaten them. A caseworker was assigned to the family, and it was decided that Gerald and Angel would stay with Monique for the time being.

Mr. Washington smiled at Gerald at the end of that very long day. "My boy Rob could learn quite a bit from you, Gerald. You got guts! And remember, you also have me. You call me if things start to get shaky, you hear?"

"I will, but we'll be fine now. I can handle Monique. She ain't like most mamas, but she's all we got. We'll do all right."

"I know you will, son. I'm sure of it."

FOURTEEN

Angel loved to dance. She wore music like a graceful gown that shimmered as she moved. Even the simplest melody became a full concert — like a music video — when Angel danced to it. And Gerald loved to watch her as she danced in her bedroom late at night, and danced in the kitchen while she was getting ready for school.

In the six years since the arrest and conviction of Jordan Sparks, music had helped Angel to heal and grow. She never had any formal dance lessons, but she made Gerald take her to every new movie that featured dancers, and she would get up in the middle of the night to watch a rerun of an old Fred Astaire movie. Whenever Angel felt sad, or guilty, or afraid, music and dancing made her feel whole again.

Life for Gerald and Angel continued to be rough even after Jordan went off to jail. Monique never did admit that she was aware of Jordan's abuse, but she did stop calling the children liars. She seemed to stop caring about the children at all.

Sometimes she went to work, but sometimes she just slept all day. They had moved four times in the last five years because Monique forgot to pay the rent. At other times she forgot to buy groceries. A caseworker checked on the children occasionally, and she tried to encourage Monique so that the family could survive. Gerald learned to cook and shop with food stamps and wash clothes at the Laundromat. He never complained about the difficulty of taking care of his little sister; rather, Angel's hugs and smiles kept him going. Gerald was her warrior and protector and she adored him.

Tiger, the kitten from that terrible Christmas six years ago, was the fat and clever ruler of wherever they lived. She ate anything — broccoli, sweet rolls, even toothpaste. She never strayed far from Angel's side and had once jumped on a dog that growled at Angel. Angel never slept without Tiger, who was the only one there to comfort her in the darkness of the night when old fears came creeping from the past.

Angel, who was now twelve, was thin and shy. She had large eyes which sometimes were full of remembered fear. Her hair was long, brown, and fuzzy. She wore it in two long braids. She walked gracefully; her movements were never quick and jerky like those of some girls her age.

At seventeen, Gerald was tough and stocky, with the muscles of a young man who knew hard work. He was dependable and strong, and storekeepers often paid him a few dollars to move boxes or clean up after hours.

Every morning, after walking Angel to her school around the corner, Gerald took the bus to Hazelwood High School. He was glad that in spite of all their moving around, he could still attend Hazelwood. He had made a couple of really good friends, and was really proud that he had made the basketball team. The Hazelwood Tigers always made the high school playoffs. Two years ago they were first in the state.

Rob's dad had called him the day after the team roster was posted. Only fifteen boys had been chosen to wear the red uniforms of the Tigers Varsity.

"Congratulations, Gerald. I'm proud of you, son."

Gerald wasn't sure if Rob's dad called everybody "son" or not, but he liked it. He'd never had a father around to call him that. "Thanks, Mr. Washington. I'm gonna do my best."

"I'll be there at the games, you know. Let me know if you ever need a ride."

"Thanks, man." Rob's dad never asked directly how things were with Gerald and Angel, but he called every few months, talking of school or baseball or the weather — letting Gerald know that he was around, just in case. Gerald never told him, but those calls meant so very much. Every year at Christmas, Mr. Washington always made sure that Angel and Gerald had something special under their tree. One year, he even provided the tree as well.

Often after basketball practice, Rob and his dad gave Gerald a ride home so that he wouldn't have to take the bus. Rob, with his natural grace and ability, was already talking of college scholarships and NBA contracts. He treated everybody as if they were his best friend, but he generally hung with Andy and Gerald and a couple of other guys from the team — Tyrone and B.J.

The basketball season had started well — they had won their first couple of games. Gerald actually looked forward to school, and even though most seventeen-year-olds would rather gag than admit they like their little sister, he let Angel tag along when she wanted, and looked forward to her cheerful smile to warm the chilly evenings at home after school.

Gerald and Angel stood at the kitchen sink together, the sunlight of a November day filtering weakly through the small window. She was washing; he was drying. The silences between them were pleasant and understood. Angel spoke first.

"When is Mama comin' home?"

"It's always hard to tell. If she got that new job, she might be real late."

"Do you think she'll let me take that dance class?"

"If she got the job, she'll be in a good mood. Ask her then."

"Gerald, you got basketball and sports and stuff. I got nothin' but the music inside of me. I want to dance!"

"Hey, the man at the chicken place around the corner said he'd let me wash dishes after school. I could get paid for what I'm doin' here!" he said, laughing. "Then you could take the dance class."

"Naw, Gerald, you stay on the team. You can't quit basketball. I think you like runnin' around in your underwear!" she replied. Gerald grinned and flicked soapy water at her. She squealed and giggled, dipped her hands in the sink, and shook her drippy fingers at his face. Gerald laughed, ducked, and just as he was chasing Angel around the kitchen with a full glass of water, Monique breezed inside with a burst of winter air.

"Ooh!" she exclaimed. "It's a freezer out there! How's my babies? And what's this water doin' all over the floor?"

Monique had not changed much in the past few years. She was still very pretty, with a tiny waist that looked good in the gold belts and shiny sashes she liked to wear. She took great pride in her hair, changing its style and color to fit her mood. Today it was a rusty blond, with a matching ponytail woven into it. Accented by bright gold earrings, her black dress and two-tone fingernails made her look much younger than she was. She looked great today — and she was smiling.

Gerald looked up at her, but his good mood was gone. He didn't like it when Monique came in smiling. He knew that Monique had probably gotten the job, which meant that she would go out tonight to "celebrate." He was proud of her that she had not returned to the drugs, but she had developed a taste for whiskey and was finding more and more excuses to go out and drink with her friends.

"Did you get the job, Mama?" asked Angel.

"Yes, baby, I did!" Monique glowed with pleasure. "I'll be answering telephones at the YMCA every day from nine to five. Aren't you proud of your mama? I gotta go celebrate!"

"That's great, Mama," Angel said, hugging her. "Uh, Mama, can I ask you something?"

"Sure, baby, what you need?"

"A lady came to my school today and she told me about this dance class that I can be in. She said I was really good. Can I be in it? Please?"

"Dancing? Probably a waste of time. How much is it gonna cost me?"

"Fifty dollars," whispered Angel, not daring to look at her mother.

"Fifty dollars! Good Lord! Hey, Gerald — has the rent been paid this month?"

"Yeah, Monique. It's been paid. Let her try it, okay?"

"Okay, baby. Go dance your little heart out! As a matter of fact, I may do a little dancin' myself tonight! I gotta go change!"

Angel grinned at Gerald. She was going to dance! A group from the Dance Theatre of Harlem was spending six weeks at her school, working with talented young people. She didn't tell Gerald that only forty children had been selected for the

110

class from over two hundred who tried out — and that only twenty of those would dance in the show at the end of the program. She had been afraid to hope.

Monique left, humming the latest song. The click of her high heels reminded Gerald of that day long ago, and he suddenly felt a little dizzy. The dishes finished, Angel took Tiger into her room and turned on the radio. She danced with her cat and danced with her dreams while Gerald wrestled with memories of pain.

FIFTEEN

"Yo! Gerald! You need a ride to the game tomorrow?" Andy yelled across the gym.

"Naw, man, I got it covered," Gerald yelled back. Andy was one of the few boys on the team with his own car. Everybody depended on him for rides, and he loved being the center of that attention. Gerald took the bus to the games. He preferred that to the noise and crowd of Andy's car. He liked the silence of the bus ride to relax him and prepare him for a really good game.

Gerald stayed every day after school for basketball practice. It was there that he felt whole and powerful. Rob, who had unanimously been named captain by the team, was tall, skinny, smart, and had the best line with girls that Gerald had ever heard. Andy was Rob's best friend. He wasn't a natural at basketball like Rob, but he tried hard and hated for Rob to outscore him. They had known each other since seventh grade and spent weekends at each other's homes. Both of them lived near the edge of the school district, where houses had neat lawns with trees in the backyard and a fresh coat of paint every other year.

Gerald no longer felt uncomfortable around them, even though he lived in an apartment building downtown that had a broken elevator, graffiti on the walls, and very little grass anywhere. Andy and Rob breezed through life, collecting friends — and never making judgments about them — with seemingly no problems at all.

Last month, after a movie one Saturday night, Andy, Rob, Tyrone, B.J., and Gerald had decided they were hungry — maybe even starving.

"What you want to eat, man? Fast food?"

"How much money you got?"

"Four dollars and eleven cents. What about you, B.J.?"

"Sixty-nine cents. Hey, Gerald, what about you?"

"I got about eight dollars."

"We rich, man. I got an idea. Let's try that new all–you–can–eat place."

"Do they really mean *all?*"

"Let's see, man!" chuckled Andy as they headed for the restaurant.

They paid for two meals, then went through the line slowly. Andy got six kinds of meat, ten dinner rolls, and four pieces of apple pie. Rob piled eight pieces of corn on the cob, a mountain of mashed potatoes, eighteen chicken wings, and three pieces of cheesecake on his plate. Tyrone picked up a stack of napkins and a bunch of silverware. They were laughing hysterically, but quietly.

"They watchin' us, man!" Gerald said fearfully.

"That's 'cause you put jelly on your potatoes, man," B.J. explained, laughing.

"We ain't done nothing wrong," Robbie said with casual confidence. "Let's just eat."

They laughed and gobbled up every bit of that food, smiling at the customers and making even the restaurant workers laugh along with them. When they finished, they cleared their plates, stood on the tables, and sang, in perfect five-part harmony, a doo-wop version of the old Drifters song "Under the Boardwalk." Everyone in the restaurant applauded and cheered as they took their bows.

An old man with dark brown skin, piercing eyes, and slick gray hair had been watching them from the back of the room. He limped over to them, gave them each a ten-dollar bill, and said seriously, "Enjoy your youth, my young friends. Tomorrow it may be gone."

Robbie thanked him, then gave his ten dollars to the busboy as a tip, and the five of them left the place, humming and happy. They ended up with a great meal, a satisfied audience, and more money than they started with. They forgot about the old man and his strange words.

B. J. Carson, as the team's manager, went to every practice and game. He was short — only about five feet tall — but he was tough and strong. He tried out for the team every year, and although he never made it, the coaches admired his courage and spirit. He loved basketball, and his sense of humor and knowledge of the game made him a natural to hang with Andy, Rob, Gerald, and Tyrone.

Sometimes taller, older kids who didn't know B.J. tried to take advantage of him. They only made that mistake once. Last year, B.J. had accidentally bumped a senior with his book bag as he walked down the hall. The senior, a six-foot six-inch, three-hundred-pound football player named Danté, had not been amused.

"Who you bumpin', punk?"

"Who you callin' punk?" B.J. had asserted without fear.

"I'm callin' you a punk, yo mama a punk, and yo greasy granny a punk too!" Danté was big and grinned cheerfully. He was used to getting his way.

B.J. put down his book bag, slowly turned around, and tensed his short, wiry frame to face the much larger boy. Danté started to laugh as B.J. crouched in a karate attack position, but his laughter stopped short as he found himself sitting on the floor in the main hallway, a calm and smiling B.J. offering his hand to help him up.

"How'd you do that, man?" asked Danté, who was more amazed than angry.

"Black belt. Master Kim. Tae kwon do. Paid for by my mama and my greasy granny," he added. "Ever need me to watch your back, call me." B.J. disappeared into the crowd. Danté just shook his head and chuckled at the nerve of the tough little guy with the powerful whip kick. He never bothered B.J. again.

The five friends had several classes together at Hazelwood High School. Rob, the smartest of them, made good grades with ease. He already had several academic and athletic scholarships lined up as possibilities. Tyrone was more interested in girls than grades, especially Rhonda, who was best friends with Andy's girlfriend, Keisha. Andy didn't make very good grades, but it seemed to Gerald that he just wanted attention at home, even attention for bad grades. Andy's parents rarely came to their games, while Rob's parents never missed one.

B.J.'s mom came to games on nights when she didn't have stuff to do at her church. Even Monique came to the big home games. Gerald never told her, but it made him feel proud.

It was Friday after the last class of the day, halfway through tenth grade, halfway through basketball season. It was raining. Gerald headed for his locker.

"Whatcha get on that math test?" Andy asked Gerald.

"Another C minus. If I study all night or don't study at all, seems like I get the same grade. I ain't seen a B in a long time."

"Don't sweat it, man. I got the lowest grade in the class — again. Coach is gonna kill me if I don't get my grades up. And my dad — he'll give me lecture number fifty-seven. You know, the one about how he always made straight A's and why can't I."

"Yeah, man," said Gerald, but he laughed to himself as he imagined Monique giving him a lecture on good grades. She never even knew when report cards came out unless he told her.

Rob and B.J. chased each other down the hall, racing to their lockers.

"And another B for B.J.!" roared B.J. as he tossed his books into his locker. Gerald threw a shoe at him, but B.J. ducked. "Too smooth for you, dude!" He grinned.

"Who we play tonight, B.J.?"

"Centerville. Easy win. Your dad comin', Rob?"

"Yeah, he'll be here."

"Can I get a ride home after the game, man?"

"Got room for me?" added Gerald.

"No sweat. What about you, Tyrone? You need a ride?"

"Naw, man. I'm gonna hang with Rhonda after the game." He grinned.

"You need a ride too, Andy? Your car still not workin'?"

"My dad said he was comin', but yeah, I'm gonna need a ride. He won't show. He's . . . Hey, Rob, that math test beat you down too?"

"Yeah, it was rough. But I got an A. Let's go to Mickey D's and get something to eat before the game." Gerald and Andy looked at each other and shook their heads. "What you gonna do, man? A man's gotta eat. Let's jet."

Every day when Gerald left practice he went by Angel's school to pick her up from dance practice. She was thriving on the hard work and sweat and hours of practice. Her face would be glowing when he picked her up, and she came home hungry and happy each day. He had watched her dance once when he got there early, and it gave him goose bumps. She was so naturally fluid and rhythmic that all she needed was the music and her body did the rest. He noticed that the instructors pointed to her with smiles of admiration.

On Friday, she was so bubbly that Gerald thought she'd explode. Her eyes were bright with excitement.

"Guess what!" She jiggled with joy.

"You won the lottery," said Gerald, smiling.

"No, silly! Better than that! I got picked to be the lead in our show next month! I get to wear a costume! Can Mama sew? How will I fix my hair? Do you think I look okay in yellow? That's what color my costume is. Do you think I'll look fat? Where am I gonna find yellow tights? The show is in only two weeks! Suppose I break my leg the night before! What is the — ?"

"Hold on there, sister! You gonna run

over me with all them questions at once! Calm down a little! I'm so proud of you! I knew you were the best!" Gerald hugged her then, tight enough to let her know how proud he was and how much he adored her.

Angel half-skipped, half-bounced the rest of the way home. She was chattering about costumes and rehearsals and the crown she would wear on her hair. Gerald only smiled and let her rattle on. He was so very proud of her, and it made him feel warm inside to know that she was truly happy at last.

Her long brown hair blew behind her in the breeze, fuzzy and never quite cooperating with brush and comb. Her eyes were sparkling and full of hope. Something in that breeze made him think of Aunt Queen, and for the first time in a very long time, he, too, felt at peace.

They climbed the six flights of stairs easily — laughing and planning for the dance recital. Angel ran through the door, calling with excitement, "Mama! I'm a star! I'm a sta— !"

Her words died. She felt as if she were choking, drowning. Sitting on the sofa, cowboy boots and all, was Jordan Sparks.

SIXTEEN

Jordan looked older, harder, and angrier. He smiled, but his eyes stayed cold and unfeeling. Monique was beside herself with excitement. She had fixed Jordan a steak dinner and an apple pie, and Monique was not known for her good cooking.

Angel screamed, ran to her room, and locked the door. Gerald, no longer an eleven-year-old kid, but a strong, muscular seventeen-year-old, looked him squarely in the face. "You ain't stayin' here! Now get out!"

Jordan didn't even blink. "Now, what kinda greetin' is that for a man who just wants to see his children?" he asked in that gravelly voice that Gerald hated.

"You ain't my daddy, and you don't deserve to be hers!"

"Oh, but I am her daddy, boy, and court says I been rehabilitated. Court says I get visitation rights. Court says you ain't got nothin' to say about that!"

"Why you got to come back here and ruin stuff? We're finally almost close to

121

happy, and you show up!" Gerald was almost in tears, but he didn't want Jordan to see him break.

"Your mama is still my wife. She done forgave me. Why can't you? I've changed, boy. I'm a new man!"

Monique seemed flustered and nervous. Jordan sat silent and staring. Finally he got up. His cowboy boots echoed loudly on the smooth wooden floor. Jordan paused at the door. "I'll be back for you tonight, Monique. Wear something pretty!"

Monique blushed and tried to hide her excitement from Gerald, who looked at her with disgust.

"And *you*," Jordan growled at Gerald, "don't mess with me. I'll be back to visit Angel. I ain't gonna hurt her. I ain't gonna even touch her. I told you I've changed. Let's shake on it like men." He offered Gerald his rough, dirty hand. Gerald didn't move.

"No," Gerald stated quietly. He walked into the other room, shaking with fury and helplessness.

Gerald wanted to spit. Instead he just ran out of the room. He knew he had to find Angel. He knocked on her door. He could hear her crying.

"It's me, Gerald. Let me in." He heard

the lock turn and he gently opened the door. Angel's eyes were glassy and un-blinking. All of the pain and memories of the past filled her so that only tears and shudders escaped her. Gerald hugged her for a long time. She quieted down gradually and was able to focus on the cat, which she stroked as she shook with swallowed sobs.

"Is he gone?" Angel asked nervously.

Gerald nodded and sighed. Angel, taking deep breaths, made sure she heard the clink of the lock in the outside door, and ran past Gerald into the bathroom. He wanted to beat something, to cry, to scream, but all he could do was listen to Angel as she threw up the way she used to, the only way she knew to purge the tension of Jordan's presence in the house.

Monique, as usual, was no help. She pretended not to notice Angel's discomfort, or Gerald's hatred. She was fluttery and excited that Jordan was back and that he still wanted her.

Gerald walked back into the living room. Jordan's cologne, which smelled to Gerald like horse sweat, hung strong and overpowering in the small room. "What's the real deal, Monique?"

"Well, Gerald, uh . . . Jordan is out and uh . . ."

"He can't stay here."

"No — I mean yes — I agree — at least for now. But you have to give him a chance, Gerald. He's changed. He's gonna try to show you. You gotta try, okay?"

"He can never be alone with Angel." Gerald's voice was hard and demanding.

"I think that's a good idea for now, Gerald. Let's see if we can all work together to make this a happy family once again."

"This was never a happy family while he was here, Monique. Your memory don't work so good, it seems."

She smiled weakly, refused to look Gerald in the eye, and went to fix her hair.

Gerald picked up the telephone.

"Hey, Rob, what's up, man? Is your dad home?"

"Yeah, he's in here acting like he knows how to fix a bathroom sink. Mom told him to call a plumber, but no, he's gotta prove he's Superman. Now we gotta brush our teeth in the kitchen sink. Hey, Dad, telephone. It's Gerald," called Rob, laughing.

"Hi, Gerald, what's up, son?"

"Hey, Mr. Washington. Sounds like you got plumbing problems."

"Nothing I can't solve. All I need is one small piece of pipe."

Gerald could hear groans of laughter coming from the background. Rob's family was always laughing about something — even Mr. Washington's mistakes. Gerald couldn't remember much laughter ever coming from his own house.

"Well, I got some bathroom problems too." Gerald paused. Rob's dad waited quietly.

"Angel's in there throwing up again. Jordan is back."

Mr. Washington gasped. "Oh, no! Has he . . . has he done anything?" he asked with severity in his voice.

"No. He's clean — so far, at least. He says he's got rights, but Angel is a nervous wreck. She can't live like this. Don't we have rights too? What can I do?"

"Look, I've got to run out and pick up this pipe. Let me come by and get you. We'll talk."

"Thanks. I'll be waiting out front."

Thirty minutes later, Mr. Washington drove up in a new blue Buick. He was dressed in jeans and a T-shirt. Actually, it was the same thing that Jordan had been wearing, but on Jordan it looked sinister and criminal. Rob's dad smiled at Gerald as he opened the car door, laugh marks making walnut brown wrinkles in the sides of his eyes.

"Is Angel okay up there?" he asked,

glancing up at the bleak and depressing apartment building.

"Yeah, she's asleep now. And Jordan won't be back for a while."

"What about Monique?"

Gerald shrugged. "Probably doing her hair for when Jordan comes by later to take her out. That's all she thinks about. She just wants to please him. She doesn't even care, or notice, how upset Angel gets."

Mr. Washington said nothing, but listened carefully.

"She wants Jordan to move back in. Can they do that?"

Mr. Washington sighed. "Probably so. Especially if Jordan doesn't do anything to get a negative report from probation."

"I heard him tell Monique that he got a job, and reports to his probation officer right on time. He even volunteers at an old-folks home once a week, just to make it look good. But I know he hasn't changed. I just know it."

"I wish I could be more help, Gerald," Mr. Washington replied with real regret. "Watch him. Try keeping a diary of his activities. It might be important later. Write down everything he does, even if it seems innocent."

"Well, at least that will give me something to do, but what about Angel?"

"Do you think Monique would let Angel spend the night at our house sometimes? She and Kiara really seem to hit it off when they're together. I know Kiara would love to have some company — there aren't any girls her age on our street."

"I don't want to be a bother."

"It's not a problem. For that matter, why don't you come and spend some time with Rob? Maybe after the game this weekend, you and Angel can come over. That will give you both a break from this mess for a little bit, and Monique can spend time alone with Jordan. I know she'll agree if you put it that way."

"Yeah, she won't care. That's the problem. She just doesn't care."

The days that followed were tense, but quiet. Jordan stopped by around dinnertime, and always left by nine o'clock. On Saturday, he stayed most of the afternoon, going to the grocery store for Monique and even sweeping the living room. He spoke to Angel only to ask her about school or dancing. Gerald watched him every moment, and true to a promise he made to himself, he never let Angel out of his sight while Jordan was there. Still, she was nervous when Jordan was there and usually threw up when he left.

SEVENTEEN

That Saturday, Angel went to Gerald's game and sat with Rob's sister Kiara. They cheered, ate popcorn, and paid more attention to the other kids than to the game. Angel and Kiara, dressed in matching jeans and shirts, walked back and forth to the refreshment stand ten or fifteen times, giggling and hoping they were being noticed. It was the first time Gerald had seen her happy since Jordan's return, and he was glad. Gerald had made several key shots early in the game and he felt like he could breathe again.

Jordan and Monique arrived late — shortly after the first quarter. Jordan's hard, sharp-toed cowboy boots clomped loudly on the wooden gym floor. People who glanced at him saw a tall, angry black man, dressed in black jeans, black T-shirt, and shiny black boots. Monique, over-dressed as usual, wore a shiny gold top with tight black stretch pants and black heels.

"He looks like a hit man," giggled Kiara

to Angel. Angel glanced at Jordan and shuddered. She did not laugh. Even across the gym, it seemed she could smell his stifling cologne.

From that moment on, Gerald had a terrible game. He was nervous and missed every shot he attempted.

"What'sa matter with you, Nickelby?" shouted the coach. "You eat rocks for dinner? Take a break. Smith, fill in for Gerald."

Gerald hated the bench, and he hated Jordan. Jordan seemed to sneer at him from across the gym, feeling Gerald's hatred and laughing at it. Monique seemed uncomfortable. She kept looking at her watch and then at Jordan to see how he was reacting, not to the game, but to her. He glanced at her once and smiled. Monique blushed with pleasure and checked her watch again. She paid no attention to Angel and Kiara. She paid no attention to the game. When the team came back on the floor after halftime, Jordan and Monique had gone.

On the way to Rob's house after the game, Gerald was silent. Angel and Kiara giggled in the backseat about boys and makeup and movie stars. He was glad she had a chance to act normal, but even Rob's good humor couldn't break him out of his deep feeling of trouble to come. Gerald knew it was only a matter of time.

The night of Angel's dance recital was stormy and overcast, but her excitement made the evening seem almost sunny. So did the garlands of flowers with which the school auditorium had been decorated for the evening. Angel had invited Kiara to the recital, and the Washingtons, since they had to drop Kiara off anyway, decided to stay. Gerald was amazed, but they looked comfortable and relaxed as they chatted with Monique while they waited for the show to begin. Monique was the one who looked agitated — and overdressed. No other mother came to the recital dressed in red sequins. She kept looking back at the door, checking for Jordan, who had promised to come.

Angel was smiling, but nervous. Her yellow costume and gold crown looked beautiful. Gerald smiled as he chatted with her by the backstage curtains. "You look like a princess, Angel. You'll do just fine. Relax."

"Do you think he'll come?" she whispered.

"I hope not," Gerald replied grimly.

130

"Is Kiara here? And Rob?" Angel really liked Rob. He could always make her laugh.

"Yeah, she's here, sitting with her mom and Monique. Rob and Andy went out with their girlfriends tonight."

"Why don't you have a girlfriend?" teased Angel.

"Me? Trouble is, I like 'em all. I haven't figured out which one is gonna be the lucky one yet."

Angel giggled and pretended to punch him. Her teacher called from backstage, and Angel blew Gerald a quick kiss. He reached out, pretended to catch the invisible kiss, smacked the side of his cheek, and grinned. She smiled at him and disappeared behind the curtain.

The crowd hushed, the lights were lowered, and the music began. Dancers filled the stage, delicately moving with the music, filling the room with magic.

"I wonder where Jordan is," muttered Monique, who spent more time watching the door than the stage.

Gerald ignored her.

"Where's Angel, Gerald?" whispered Kiara, who was sitting on his other side.

"Sh-sh-sh. Here she comes."

The stage was dark for a moment, and

silent; then suddenly, with a burst of golden light and an orchestral overture from the CD player behind the curtain, Angel stepped onto the stage.

The story she danced was about a lost child, a child who feared the darkness but found the light with the help of the wind and the stars. It was as if the dance had been created just for her. As she danced, Gerald could feel her pain; he could see her fear and misery. The music was her voice, and the dance was her only means of escape.

When the music finally stopped, the audience reacted with stunned silence; the dance had been so beautiful and expressive. Gradually, the applause grew from very small to a thunderous standing ovation for the little girl who took her bows with tears in her eyes.

Gerald was so proud of her he was about to explode. He clapped so hard that his hands hurt. He cheered. He whistled. He stomped his feet.

"Wow, Gerald!" shouted Mr. Washington over the deafening applause. "I didn't know she was such a beautifully talented girl. We're so glad we came."

Kiara, who hadn't really been into ballet,

cheered as well, admiring her new friend's talents. Angel was going to spend the night with Kiara after the show. Her parents had promised they could go get ice cream, rent a video, and sleep as late as they wanted the next morning.

Monique clapped also, but she seemed nervous and kept looking over her shoulder toward the back of the auditorium. Jordan had not arrived.

"He'll be sorry he missed this," she whispered to Gerald.

"I'm glad he did. It would dirty a beautiful moment for Angel."

"Don't be so mean, Gerald. Hasn't he been a perfect gentleman since he's been out? Hasn't he tried to show you that he's sorry and he's changed? You gotta learn to forgive and forget!"

Gerald sighed. Monique would never see, because she didn't want to see. Yes, Jordan had been acting perfectly. But Gerald was sure that it was just that — an act. He did not trust Jordan Sparks.

EIGHTEEN

When school let out for the summer, Monique let Jordan move back into the apartment. Angel was sullen and quiet; Gerald was angry, but helpless. Jordan went out of his way to be polite and nonthreatening. In the five months since he had gotten out of prison, he had not touched Gerald, hadn't even raised his voice. And he had stayed very clear of Angel, speaking to her only to praise her or ask her questions. Monique was extremely happy, for not only was Jordan moving back, but he seemed to be the man that she had always dreamed he could be.

Angel talked to Kiara on the phone almost daily, and that seemed to help her depression and concern. She no longer threw up every day, but she stayed nervous and tense.

It was hot in the small apartment and Gerald was restless. He wanted to go play basketball with his friends, but he was afraid to leave the house. While he felt it was his job to protect Angel, he also needed to get out.

134

"Monique, I'm gonna go hoop for a little bit. You keep an eye out for Angel for me?"

"Sure, Gerald. Go ahead. You worry too much. She'll be fine. I'll make sure. Go — have some fun with your friends." She was watching TV. Jordan was not there.

Gerald let Angel know he was going. She looked a little worried, but she told him, "Get out of here. You can't stay here for the rest of your life lookin' out for me. I can take care of myself. And besides, he *has* been behaving himself." She sighed. "When I grow up and become a famous dancer, I'm gonna move far, far away from here."

Gerald smiled at her and left, dribbling his basketball, wishing he could bounce all of his fears and troubles away. He played for a couple of hours and returned, hot and sweaty, but more relaxed. He decided to take a cool shower and maybe look for a job in the morning.

When Gerald reached the apartment, the door was open and he could see nothing but dark silence. His heart began to beat faster as he tiptoed into the darkness. No sound, no light, no movement.

"Angel?" he whispered softly. "Monique?" Nothing.

Gerald was so scared he felt sick. *If something has happened to Angel,* Gerald thought, *I'll go crazy!*

Why had he left the house? What could have happened? Where was everybody? And where was Jordan Sparks?

Gerald almost ran to Angel's bedroom, feeling his way in the darkness. He was so afraid, so very afraid of what he might find. "Angel!" he screamed in fear. "Angel! Where are you?"

"I'm over here, Gerald," called Angel's voice. "I'm okay. The electricity went off and me and Tiger were just sitting here in the dark, trying not to be scared."

Relieved, Gerald began to breathe again. "But where's Monique?"

"Oh, she said she had to get some cigarettes for Jordan. She left just before the lights went off. She said she'd be right back, but she's been gone for over an hour, I think."

"Has Jordan been here?" asked Gerald, just to make sure.

"No, he's been out all evening, thank goodness. Just me and Tiger. I'm glad you're home. I was scared."

"Me too. Can you imagine what I thought when I saw the door standing open and the lights off? I wonder why Monique didn't remember to shut and lock the door."

"You know how she is when she's around Jordan," Angel replied. "She gets so excited and flustered. He called and said he'd be home by midnight and he wanted her to go get him some cigarettes. Why can't he go and get his own stupid smokes?"

As she spoke, the power was restored and the lights came back on. Gerald and Angel grinned at each other, just a little ashamed of their fears of the darkness. It was then that Gerald became aware of the sirens.

Fire and emergency sirens were commonplace in the neighborhood — the city's largest hospital was just around the corner. But sirens in the distance and sirens right on the corner have two different sounds. These sirens were close.

Gerald looked out of their sixth-floor window. He couldn't see much. "You and Tiger stay here, Angel. And lock the door when I leave. I'm going downstairs to see what's going on. Something has happened on the corner. I'll be right back."

Angel nodded. As Gerald ran down the six flights of steps, his fear expanded like a balloon in his chest. A crowd had already gathered by the time he reached the corner. A tall, bearded taxi driver stood weeping in the street. "I didn't see her. I didn't see her," he kept repeating. "She was running — like she was in a hurry! She ran right in front of me! I didn't see her. I swear I didn't see her!"

The paramedics were lifting the victim into the ambulance. She did not seem to be breathing. It was Monique. Clutched in one hand was a pack of cigarettes.

"Does anybody know this lady?" a policeman asked the crowd.

Gerald's voice at first failed him. He finally spoke loud enough to be heard. "She's my mother," he said helplessly.

NINETEEN

Angel woke up screaming. "Mama!" she gasped.

Gerald, asleep in the next room, ran to Angel immediately. "It's okay, Angel. Mama is gonna be okay. It's just gonna take some time. Now go back to sleep. It's three in the morning."

Angel relaxed a bit and went back to sleep. She often had episodes like this since the accident. Gerald watched her for a few minutes before he turned off her light. She had grown thinner and was almost a waxy pale. He thought she might need a doctor. What he knew she needed was some stability and a release from fear.

Monique had not been killed that night two weeks ago. Although most of her injuries were around her face and head, she had quickly regained consciousness. She seemed dazed and confused, but was well enough to ask about Jordan.

"You seen Jordan? Is he okay?"

"He's not here, Monique. He doesn't even know you're here. I don't know where

139

he is," replied Gerald curtly.

"How'd you get here? Where's Angel?" Monique looked confused.

"I'm here, Mama," Angel said tearfully. "We rode in the ambulance. Don't you remember?"

"No. Uh, when you see Jordan, tell him . . . tell him . . ." She faded into sleep again. Gerald looked at Angel and smiled grimly.

"Well, at least we know she's okay. Are you all right?"

Angel nodded, but she was jumpy and anxious. When she ran to the bathroom suddenly, Gerald knew that she was more upset than she wanted to admit. She was vomiting again.

Monique was released the next morning. Jordan never even bothered to come to the hospital. When Angel and Gerald helped the weakened Monique walk up the six flights of steps, they found Jordan half asleep on the living room couch.

"How you feel, Monique?" he inquired sleepily. "Neighbor told me what happened. I was just on my way down to the hospital. How'd you get home?"

Gerald and Angel stared coldly at Jordan and refused to answer. Monique, still fluttery in spite of her injuries, smiled at him from under her head bandage and told him, "Ms. Walker next door gave me a ride. No problem. I knew you were coming. See, kids — I told you he was coming."

Angel and Gerald said nothing.

Suddenly Monique looked around wildly. "Gerald! What happened to them cigarettes? I remember now. I went to get cigarettes for you, Jordan. I bet them ambulance men took them cigarettes. I'm sorry, Jordan. I got 'em for you just like you said."

"It's okay, baby," Jordan crooned in his rocky voice. "You can get me some more another time, when you get better. Come sit here by me." He patted a spot on the sofa.

Monique grinned with relief and happiness. Jordan glanced at Gerald as he put his arm around her, and gave him a hard, cold smile that said, "I can do anything I want. You can't stop me."

Gerald, helpless for the moment, looked away, but he thought, *Maybe you're wrong, Jordan Sparks. You just might be wrong.*

Several days after the accident, Angel sat in a corner of her bedroom, stroking her cat and staring silently into space. Even Gerald couldn't get her to smile.

"Come on, Angel, Monique could be

141

dead. She's just hurt and she's healing slowly — I think from the inside out. Give it time."

Angel sighed. "If she dies . . . doesn't make it, Gerald, all we got is Jordan. I can't bear to even think about it, and that's all I been doing lately."

"Monique is not gonna die," Gerald told her firmly. "If she was gonna die, that taxi woulda killed her!"

Angel just stared out of the window and stroked her sleeping cat. Finally Gerald had an idea. He put a tape into her little cassette player and pushed PLAY. It was the music to the dance she'd performed just a few months before. Angel at first refused to notice, but as the beauty of the music grew in intensity, all of the pain and memories of her past grew within her. She wept. She cried until she had no tears left. Finally, she stood up and moved lightly to the final strains of the melody.

"Thanks, Gerald," she said quietly. "I'm gonna be okay."

"I know, Angel. You know you always got me."

She smiled at him. "Yeah, I know that. But first I gotta make sure I got hold of *me*."

"What about Jordan?" Gerald asked her.

"Looks like we're stuck with him, at least for now."

"I think he really cares about Mama, in his own twisted way. He seems like he's trying to do right, and he doesn't bother me anymore, so we'll just have to wait and see."

"Yeah, but I still don't trust him."

"Me neither," Angel replied with a shudder.

Rob's father called a couple of weeks after the accident.

"What's up, Gerald? How's your mom?"

"Well, the cuts and bruises have healed mostly, but she's like not all here yet. She's like a shadow instead of a real person."

"What do you mean?"

"It's like part of her is sorta unplugged. She knows us, and talks to us, but it seems like she's always floating somewhere . . . else. It's hard to put into words."

"Is she in any pain?"

"She keeps insisting that her head hurts or her back is on fire, but that's only when she runs out of her pain pills. Jordan kept her supplied with refills of her prescription, and when the doctor wouldn't give her any more, he brought these weird-lookin' shiny red pills and these bright blue-and-yellow pills that I ain't never seen before."

"Sounds like she's starting on another problem, Gerald."

"Yeah, I know. She's been straight for years. I think the accident gave her an excuse to start using again. I don't think she even knows what's happening."

"These things take time, Gerald. And remember, you can't solve your mother's problems. Is she okay by herself during the day?"

"Yeah, she watches TV most of the day, just sitting here like a piece of furniture, except for the talk shows. She likes those. Sometimes she'll just laugh out loud at those outrageous folks who tell their private stuff to the world."

"What about Jordan?"

"Well, only when Jordan comes home does it seem like she lights up a little. She combs her hair and changes her dress, but then it seems like she forgets why she did it. Then she cries — unless he's brought her some more pills. Then she's silly for a couple of hours before she passes out in front of the TV."

"How does Jordan take that?"

"Jordan seems uncomfortable around her. I think he gives her the pills so he won't have to deal with her at all. He found another job, working nights, which me and Angel think is cool. We both sleep good at night because of it."

"Angel hasn't called Kiara much lately. How's she doing?"

"It's hard to tell. Angel cries a lot too, but I don't know how much of that is teenage girl stuff and how much is because Monique is all messed up."

"But Jordan's not . . . bothering her?"

"No," Gerald said with a sigh, "at least that's not a problem right now. But Jordan isn't happy, and that's not good."

"Why don't you and Angel come over this weekend. It's been a while."

"Thanks, man, but I gotta keep an eye on Monique. Maybe Angel can come. She hasn't seen Kiara since school started."

"Kiara is pulling on the phone. She wants to talk to Angel. In the meantime, take care, Gerald. Call me anytime. You know that."

"Yeah, man. Thanks." Gerald sighed and held the phone out to Angel. "Hey Angel — telephone. It's Kiara."

"What's up, girl?" Kiara asked when Angel got on the telephone.

"Not much."

"How's your mom?"

"She's not bleeding or anything, but all she does is sit and watch TV. Her mind kinda fades in and out, if you know what I mean. I think she's takin' too many of those painkillers the doctors gave her."

"Do you think it's gonna get better?"

"Yeah, the doctor told Gerald that she'd be back to normal in a few months, but I sorta miss her, you know — the way she used to be?"

"Yeah, I hear you. Your mom always had it together. Her nails, her hair, *and* her shoes always matched!"

Angel laughed. "You got that right. And her clothes! Remember that time she went to work and we tried on all those dresses with the sparkles and the sequins? My mama was a real fancy lady."

"She still is, Angel," Kiara reminded her. "She's gonna be back like she was. You'll see."

"Yeah, I hope so. You know, even though she wasn't always the best mother in the world, she's all I got." Angel started to cry.

"It's gonna be okay, Angel. It's gonna be okay," Kiara soothed her friend over the phone. "You want to come over this weekend?"

"Yeah, that'll be cool."

"I'll see if my dad can pick you up."

"Thanks, Kiara. I'm glad I got somebody to talk to."

"Hey, you can tell me anything, girl. Peace."

No, not everything, Angel thought as she hung up the phone. Some things had to stay in the secret places.

TWENTY

October was unusually hot. The temperature stayed in the 90s every day. School was unbearable for Gerald and Angel, and when they got home, the small apartment was hot and miserable. The electricity went out almost weekly — power surges, the electric company said.

After school, it was too hot to play basketball, too hot to dance, too hot even to eat. Angel had a small fan in her room. Gerald had nothing but whatever breeze decided to find his window. Monique and Jordan's room had a small window air conditioner, but she kept the door closed, watching what Gerald called "the parade of weirdos" on the talk shows. Even when the power went off, Monique sat in front of the TV. Sometimes she laughed at the dull, empty screen. She wasn't getting much better. She used beer now, instead of water, to wash down the pills that Jordan brought her.

"Here, Monique, drink some ice water," Gerald said to her. "It will keep you cool in all this heat."

"Water makes me gag," Monique said without taking her eyes from the TV screen. "Bring me another beer. It settles my stomach. And one of those red pills from the doctor. Gotta do what the doctor said."

Gerald sighed and left the ice water next to her bed. He knew she would get up and get the beer herself while the ice slowly melted in the water glass.

Jordan hated the heat. He stayed in their room, ignoring Monique and her nonstop television, with the air conditioner turned up as high as it could get and blowing directly on him. When the power went out, he cursed and fussed and left the apartment in a fury, heading for a bar where he could sit in cool air, sipping cold drinks.

The trouble began on an especially hot Saturday. Angel usually enjoyed Saturday mornings because she had them to herself. Jordan, who was working days now, had gone to work, and Gerald had found a part-time job at the fried-chicken store around the corner. She would turn the music up really loud and dance through the apartment, with Tiger her only audience.

Jordan slammed open the front door, cursing the heat and cursing his job. He

149

kicked the cat as it scurried to get out of his way. Angel looked up, alarmed, and ran to her bedroom. She heard Jordan yank open his bedroom door with fury. It was then that she heard him bellow, "WHO STOLE MY AIR CONDITIONER?"

Monique smiled sweetly when she saw Jordan, totally unaware of his raging anger.

"MONIQUE! YOU WITLESS IDIOT! WHAT DID YOU DO TO MY AIR CONDITIONER?"

She glanced over to the gaping hole where the air-conditioning unit had been, and gasped. She hadn't even noticed that it was gone. Monique looked confused and tried to remember, but gave up with a small shrug of her shoulders, then headed back toward her favorite chair to watch TV.

"I don't know, Jordan. I'm sorry. I should have watched it better. I'm sorr—"

Jordan could take no more. He raised his arm above his head and slapped Monique with the back of his hand so hard that she fell onto the bed. Pain and confusion filled her face as she reached up to feel her bruised and bleeding lip.

"I said I was sorry," she mumbled through her tears.

Jordan looked at her with disgust and

stomped out of the room.

Angel peeked her head out of her door, but darted back in when she saw the look on Jordan's face. He was purple with rage. He stormed across the room and got to his bedroom door just as Gerald was coming back from his job. His fist hit Gerald full in the face. Blood spurted from Gerald's nose and lip as he staggered to the floor.

"THAT'LL TEACH YOU TO STEAL MY STUFF!" Jordan roared at Gerald as he left. The sound of his cowboy boots on the steps thundered, then gradually faded away.

Gerald sat on the floor, stunned. Angel ran from her room. "Are you okay?" she asked fearfully.

"Yeah, I think so," replied Gerald, who was getting more angry than scared. "What set his fire off?"

"Somebody stole his air conditioner from the window."

"So let him sweat like the rest of us," Gerald retorted.

"I wonder if he got into some trouble at his job," Angel added. "He's home so early."

"I hope he didn't get fired," groaned Gerald. "That means big trouble."

Gerald went to the bathroom and wiped

the blood from his nose, which was bleeding but did not seem to be broken. He was angry — hot, seething angry — but he knew that, because of Angel, he had to control himself. He also knew that a final showdown with Jordan had to come.

Monique emerged from the bedroom then, lips bloody and face swollen from crying.

"Mama!" Angel screamed. "I didn't know he hit you too. Mama, are you okay?"

"Sure, baby, I'm fine, I'm fine. You know what? I didn't like that! I didn't like that at all."

"Monique, here's a washcloth. Wash your face. Are you gonna be okay? Should I call the doctor?" Gerald asked.

Monique washed her face obediently. She looked as if she had just awakened from a terrible nightmare. "No, I didn't like that at all," she repeated. "I don't think I'm gonna let him hit me anymore. Did he hit you too, Gerald? That's not good, not very good. No, we're not gonna let him do this anymore."

Angel and Gerald looked at each other in amazement. Monique was almost making sense. She still didn't sound quite normal, but she was making some kind of sense. Maybe Jordan's slap had made her come to her senses.

Angel hugged her mother. "We gonna be okay, Mama?"

"We gonna be okay, baby," Monique repeated. Angel hoped that Monique was really on the way back to her. Monique smiled at her daughter. The moment faded.

"Almost time for *Police Patrol*," Monique said suddenly. "My lip hurts. Where did I put those pills?" She wandered back into the bedroom.

Angel sighed in disappointment and let Monique return to the bedroom and the TV.

"She's getting better, Angel," Gerald said with a touch of enthusiasm. "If we can flush those pills down the toilet, she might be okay. In the meantime, speaking of that TV show, do you think we should call the police?"

Angel thought for a moment. "Are you hurt?"

"Not really," Gerald admitted. "But he had no business hitting me, and I'm sure not gonna let him hit Monique again. Suppose he decides to hit you next time?"

Angel considered carefully. "Is Monique hurt?" she asked Gerald.

"I think she's all right, but her lip is gonna take a day or two to heal."

"Let's think this thing out. If we call the police, they will take Jordan away."

"Good," Gerald replied with force.

"Maybe not," Angel said thoughtfully. "How long will he stay in jail? A week? A month? And what will he do to get back at us when he gets out? And he *will* get out."

Gerald looked at Angel in amazement and admiration. At thirteen, she was really pretty, with her golden-brown skin and long, slightly fuzzy ponytail that she liked to toss as she walked. The problems of the past had given her a toughness and strength that most girls her age had yet to find. "So you think we shouldn't call the police?" he asked her. Gerald was used to making the decisions for all of them. It was a good feeling to be able to listen to her input.

"I'm not sure. I just think that right now, we need the money he's bringin' in. Mama's not quite right yet. She's probably not even capable of filing charges. There's no telling where her mind might be when the police get here. They might take her away, too, and split me and you up. I couldn't deal with that."

"Okay," Gerald said slowly. "No police

this time. But he gets no more chances. I just hope we've made the right decision."

"Me too," she added with fear in her voice. "Me too."

TWENTY-ONE

Jordan did not return until the next morning. Monique refused to smile at him this time. She rolled her eyes, frowned at him, and refused even to speak. She turned the TV up as loud as it would go and ignored him.

He looked at Gerald, but did not apologize. Jordan had bought doughnuts and milk, along with fresh fruit and a dozen eggs. Angel unpacked the groceries quietly. Except for the blaring of the TV coming from Monique's room, all was silent. Jordan knew that they had not called the police. He knew that they should have, and he understood why they didn't. He accepted the silent conversation, agreeing to their unspoken terms. They understood each other. The incident was not mentioned again.

Jordan found another job, sweeping up in a factory, but he hated it, and was tense, restless, and irritable. Gerald was surprised he stayed around. Monique had many good days now. Gerald and Angel watered down her beer, and when she asked for her pills, they brought her multivitamins instead. Gerald had flushed the pills Jordan brought her. He and Angel had cheered as they circled down to the sewer where they belonged. Monique never even noticed the switch. She was like a flower that had been battered by a storm, but not quite destroyed. Gradually, she began to strengthen and bloom again.

"Isn't it time for basketball, Gerald?" she asked one day.

"Yeah," he answered with surprise. "We practice every day."

"I remember," she replied foggily. "You play for the Lions."

"No, Monique, but you're close. It's the Tigers. The Hazelwood Tigers."

"Oh, yeah." She smiled vaguely. "Tigers."

Gerald was a starter this basketball season along with Robbie Washington and Andy Jackson. He felt good about himself for the first time in a long time. Rob's dad came to every game and cheered them all on. Angel was dancing again, Monique faded away less often, and Jordan, although always tense and irritable, left them alone.

Gerald looked forward to his basketball games, for the physical release, and when he could he liked to hang with the boys on the team. He didn't have many friends, so Andy, Rob, and B.J. meant a lot to him, although he never told them. Angel stayed with a neighbor until Gerald got home, but he didn't like to stay out too late. He still didn't trust Jordan.

The game of November 7 went well. Gerald felt relaxed, and although he was nowhere near the high scorer, he had played one of his best games.

"Hey, Gerald, what's up, man?" asked Rob as he changed his shoes.

"Nothin' much — cold-blooded game, Rob. Twenty-seven points — you be dealin' out there!" Gerald replied with real admiration.

"What can I say? College scouts from all over the world are knockin' on my door, beggin' me to drive six new Cadillacs to their school, to instruct the women in the dorms on the finer points of, shall we say, scorin', and to teach skinny little farm boys what it is!"

Gerald laughed at Rob's usual foolishness. "Andy, I don't see why you hang with this big-head fool, except maybe to learn some basketball. What you score tonight — four?"

"Hey, Gerald, I thought you was my man. You sound like the coach — and it was six points, thank you. I got more important things on my mind tonight," added Andy with fake dignity.

"Yeah, maybe Keisha can teach him some basketball!" teased Rob. "You wanna go with us tonight, Gerald? We got some brew and we just gonna be chillin'."

"Naw, Rob. I got to be gettin' home to check on my little sister. And my old man . . . you know how he is. . . . Besides, who would wanna be seen with two dudes named after a couple of dead presidents anyway?" Gerald laughed as he packed up his gym bag.

"Forget you, man. You seen B.J. and Tyrone?" Rob asked.

"Yeah, man. They waitin' for you out by Andy's car."

"Hey, Andy, when you gonna get that raggedy red car of yours painted?" Rob yelled across the locker room.

"When my old man gets tired of lookin' at it, I guess," Andy yelled back, laughing. "He said something about a reward if my grades get better, but you know how that is."

"Yeah, man. Parents be trippin'. Still, at least you got a car. But don't get me talkin' 'bout fathers. He's the reason why I gotta raise outta here now. Where y'all goin'?" Gerald asked.

"No particular place. We just gonna chill." Andy grinned. "We might try to find a party, or we might just finish off them beers and let the party find us. Then I'm headin' over to Keisha's house, after I take these turkeys home."

"Don't let Keisha find out you been drinkin'. You know she'll go off!"

"Not to worry, Gerald, my man. Not to worry. I'm outta here! Peace."

Gerald caught the first bus and was probably home before Andy and Rob had finished their first six-pack. Jordan was still at work, so Gerald got Angel from next door and fixed them both a couple of Aunt Queen's "scramburglers." They were watching the late news when the phone rang.

"Gerald, this is Keisha. Have you seen Andy?"

"Naw, I went home right after the game, but Andy and Rob, and I think Tyrone and B.J. too, left together in Andy's car. Andy said he was comin' by your house after he took those clowns home. He ain't there yet?"

"No. Well, if he calls you, tell him to get in touch with me right away, okay? Hey, you haven't heard anything about any accidents, have you?"

"Why is it the first thing a girl thinks about if her boyfriend is late is that he's been in an accident? I bet he's in the backseat of his car, kissin' all over some real sexy woman!"

"All you fellas are alike — worthless. Call me if you hear anything, okay?"

"Sure. Later."

Gerald knew that Andy, Rob, and Tyrone were planning to drink tonight after the game. Keisha's call had him a little worried. Andy was silly, but he wasn't stupid. Besides, they were only seventeen. What could possibly happen?

Gerald sat next to the phone, thinking about how things had gradually changed since last year. Sure, Andy was still silly, making yo-yo grades, Rob was still the best player on the team, Tyrone spent most of his time with Rhonda, and B.J. was still short. But now Andy drove to school every day. Gerald thought it was odd that of the four of them, Andy, who had the worst grades, was the only one who had been given a car by his folks. Andy's parents rarely came to their games, but Andy always had plenty of money to spend, on food, on the latest CDs — and on beer.

Most of the boys — all except B.J. — had started drinking. At parties, after

161

games, after school — beer was easy to get and felt better than soda pop on a Saturday night. Even Gerald, who had seen up close the awful things a drunken man can do, would split a six-pack with Andy and Rob. It made him feel strong and in charge of his life. He was tired of being scared and depressed and worried all the time. The beer made him forget. He liked that. Rob's dad didn't know and Andy's dad didn't notice, so splitting a few beers after a game had become routine. *They can handle it,* Gerald thought. *They probably just found a new place to party tonight. Girls worry too much.*

But when he didn't hear anything more after an hour, he called Keisha back. Her dad's answering machine picked up. B.J.'s line was busy. So was Andy's. There was no answer at Rob's house. Finally, he reached Rhonda.

"Hey, Rhonda, what's up? Keisha called me lookin' for Andy. You seen him?"

"No, Gerald. Didn't anybody call you? There was an accident. Rob was . . . Rob was . . . Rob's dead! Andy ran into a wall, there was an explosion, and they all got out except for Rob. Rob's dead! I can't deal with this! I feel like I'm gonna explode!"

Gerald hung up the phone and sat down

in a heap on the floor. He was too stunned to even cry. He was sitting there shaking when Angel walked into the room.

"What's wrong, Gerald?" she asked gently.

Gerald could barely breathe. All of the pain of the past crowded in on him — Aunt Queen's death, Monique's accident, Jordan's abuses. He sobbed finally with huge, burning explosions of pain. He wept for several minutes. Angel sat next to him, feeling his sorrow, understanding his grief.

"It coulda been me. They wanted me to come with them tonight, but I didn't. And now Rob's dead. It coulda been me. It coulda been me."

Angel's tears dripped softly onto the cold wooden floor. "Not Robbie. Oh, please, not Robbie!" Gerald couldn't help her this time. His own grief threatened to strangle him.

Robbie can't be dead! Robbie can't be dead! Gerald repeated wordlessly to himself. *Not Robbie. Not cool, silly, fun-loving Rob!* Gerald felt weak and heavy. He felt like he couldn't breathe, like a stone wall was sitting on his chest with the bricks running through his veins. Nothing worked right or felt normal.

He couldn't cry any more. He could only hold his head between his arms to try and block the vision that slipped in anyway. The fire — the screams — the silence.

Gerald suddenly shuddered. "What about Rob's dad? I been so busy trying to make this fit inside my head that I forgot all about Robbie's family. Oh, my God! They must be ripped!"

Gerald ran to the phone and punched the numbers with fear and ferocity. The pleasant voice of the answering machine that never had to feel sorrow or pain answered cheerfully, "You have reached the Washington residence. Please leave your number, and have a nice day!" Gerald hung up in despair. He didn't think he would ever have another nice day as long as he lived.

"Angel, I gotta go over there. Rob's dad was there for me. I gotta go!"

"Let me go with you. Kiara's going to need someone who knows how to cry. And that's one thing I know about. You got bus money?"

"Yeah, let's go."

Gerald and Angel walked from the bus stop in silence. It was late — well after midnight — and the stars sparkled faintly above the streetlight.

Angel glanced up. "How can the stars still shine, Gerald?"

"I don't know. It seems like the world ought to stop or something — like they ought to not show up tonight at least."

"How can the world keep on going like nothing's happened?"

They walked up to Rob's driveway just as the Washingtons were pulling in. Kiara's door opened slowly, but she just sat there. Angel walked over to the car and offered her hand. Kiara reached toward her hesitantly and touched Angel's trembling fingers. She got out then and collapsed in huge sobs in her friend's arms.

Angel, standing under the shadow of Rob's basketball net on the garage door, glanced at the uncaring stars and waited until Kiara's storm was reduced to sniffles and sobs.

Rob's mom walked unsteadily to the house, let the dog out, took the mail from the mailbox, and after finishing with the meaningless details of the moment, sat down on the front steps, shivering and helpless. Mr. Washington picked up Rob's basketball and held it in his hands, staring at its roundness, feeling the ridges and lumps on it, softly repeating Rob's name.

"Robbie, Robbie, Robbie, Robbie, Robbie . . ."

Gerald walked over to him and placed

his hand on the older man's shoulder, just as Rob's dad had done for him on that day that now seemed so long ago. Mr. Washington trembled and touched Gerald's hand. His eyes said thanks, but his lips could not yet speak; too many other words and thoughts were crowded in his mind that evening. He went to his wife and took her hand, and together they walked over to Kiara. The three of them glanced at the basketball net and Rob's father let the ball drop with a dull thud to the driveway. It rolled to Gerald's feet. Gerald picked it up slowly. Holding it seemed to help erase some of the confusion that clogged his mind.

"Can I hold on to this for a little?" he asked hesitantly.

"Please do," answered Mr. Washington huskily. "He would want . . ."

Rob's father finally wept. Mrs. Washington and Kiara took him into the house then.

Mrs. Washington glanced back. "I'm sorry," she said to Gerald. "Did you and Angel want to stay over?"

"Oh no! We just came to be with you all for a little bit. We gotta get back home now. Call us. We'll be around."

Rob's mom smiled, then closed the door

softly behind her. Gerald and Angel walked silently into the darkness, back to the darkness of their own home.

TWENTY-TWO

Robbie Washington's funeral was held on a Saturday. More than five hundred teachers, students, parents, and friends attended. Andy, the driver of the car, sat bandaged and dazed in the third row. Gerald, consumed with grief, sat silently next to Andy, consumed with guilt. *Pain is lonesome*, thought Gerald as he watched all the kids at school caught up in their grief. *You gotta deal with it all alone.* Gerald noticed with anger that neither of Andy's parents had come to the funeral.

During the recessional, Rob's mother stopped for a moment at the third row. She glanced at Gerald with brief despair, and moved on. She would not even look at Andy.

After Rob's funeral, Gerald wanted to quit the basketball team. It was no longer any fun without Rob's silliness and Andy's teasing competition with Rob for points, for food, even for girls. Andy took Rob's death the hardest. He and Robbie had been so close, and he could not overcome feeling responsible for Rob's death. Although most of the kids at school were understanding, some of them also had trouble with it. Andy found the word "killer" taped to his locker one day.

Coach Ripley thought that keeping the team together and finishing the season would help to save them all. Andy was made captain of the team in Rob's place. Gerald knew that Andy was proud, but that he felt uncomfortable as well. Andy knew he couldn't fill Rob's shoes. He wasn't sleeping well and his grades, which were never very good, got even worse. His parents sent him to a psychologist for counseling, which seemed to help a bit, but Gerald could see how much he was hurting.

Gerald knew about hurt. He lived with it all the time. His life, from the moment his mother had abandoned him when he was three, had been a series of disappointments and hardships, but he managed to keep his head above water most of the time. And whenever he felt like sinking, he had Angel to hold him up.

But Rob's death was different. Rob was young and talented and had a bright future. He'd had two parents who adored him, not at all like the abusive Jordan and helpless

Monique. Gerald couldn't understand why Rob was gone and he still lived. He started coming home late from games, walking the five miles instead of riding the bus. He felt like he couldn't breathe on the bus anymore. Walking helped him to think and to clear the confusion in his head.

Entering the apartment around midnight one night, Gerald was surprised to see Angel there, with Jordan.

"What are you doing here?" he growled at Jordan.

"I live here."

"I always get Angel from Miss Martin's house," stated Gerald with suspicion.

"Miss Martin had to leave," Jordan replied.

"It's okay, Gerald," Angel added, to reassure him. "Jordan took me to get something to eat. Everything is fine."

Gerald didn't like it, but he said nothing. He went to sleep, exhausted, and slept without dreaming.

Angel woke Gerald the next morning with a surprise. It was Saturday, and she knew he had two tournament games to play, so she had fixed him some lumpy grits and a piece of toast with cherry jelly. He grinned at her.

"Why you being so nice?"

" 'Cause you been funky blue since Rob

170

died. I thought you needed some cheering up." Angel, at thirteen, was thin and reserved, but when she smiled, her eyes revealed a glow she rarely displayed otherwise.

"Any problem with Jordan?" asked Gerald as he licked his fingers.

Angel sighed. Her smile faded a bit. "No, not at all. He's been polite and calm for weeks now. He spends a lot of time at the bar down the street and he doesn't even look at me anymore. I think that bad stuff is over. I think he's trying, at least."

"Well, I still don't trust him. As soon as I graduate from high school, me and you are gettin' out of here!"

"Where will we go?" Angel asked with a little fear. "And what about Mama?"

"Maybe Monique has already left *us*," Gerald mused. "But we can live somewhere far away from Jordan Sparks!"

Angel didn't see any way out. She glanced down with resignation. "We're stuck here for a while," she said quietly.

"Maybe. Hey, how's your dancing?"

She grinned again. "Delicious! We have a spring show coming up. I think I'm gonna get the lead! Will you come see me?"

"Well, I may be busy — there's a rerun

of a Frisbee tournament that I may want to catch on TV. . . ." She took one of his pillows and popped him on his head. He grabbed the other pillow and they chased each other, screaming and laughing, through the house. They didn't even notice when Jordan's door opened.

"What's all that foolishness!" he yelled.

"Sorry," said Angel, suddenly quiet.

Amazingly, Jordan smiled. "No problem," he said. "Just don't wake up the neighbors."

Gerald and Angel looked at each other with disbelief. Jordan closed his door. "Maybe I was right," said Angel with quiet hope. Gerald said nothing.

Gerald left for the basketball tournament feeling better than he had in a long time. The sky was clear and the air was fresh and chilly. Angel had dance lessons, or he would have taken her with him. But she seemed relaxed and knew to go to Miss Martin's apartment after dance.

Angel got home late in the afternoon, humming with excitement and happiness. She bounced up the stairs, her light steps barely touching them. She knocked on Miss Martin's door, but it was locked and no one answered. Puzzled, but not concerned, Angel went to her own apartment.

No one, not even Monique, was home — just the way she liked it. She got a couple of hot dogs out of the refrigerator and put them in a pot on the stove to boil.

Waiting for the hot dogs, she put in a cassette and turned the music up loud. She was dancing the steps of the lead part, practicing the part she *knew* she'd get. She heard only the music, only the beautiful music. She did not hear Jordan enter the room.

She smelled him before she heard him, before she saw him. He had been drinking. Heavily. His eyes were red and glassy. His lips were parted, and his breath reeked with foul, sour fumes. Angel was more surprised than afraid. It had only been a few hours before that Jordan had actually been smiling.

He was smiling once again — but it was the smile of the monster that lived within Jordan Sparks.

Angel, who was starting to feel the danger of the situation, started to back toward the door. She wished she had run out when he'd first walked in, but she had stopped being wary, stopped being afraid. By losing her fear, she had lost her chance.

"Where's Mama?" Angel asked warily.

"She ain't here." He walked toward her.

"Don't start, Jordan. Please." Angel was beginning to feel dizzy.

Jordan lurched forward and grabbed her arm. "You think you pretty cute, don't you?"

"No, Jordan, just let me go. Let me fix you something to eat."

"I ain't hungry. I want some . . . some female companionship. I ain't even talked to a woman since your mama run like a fool in front of that car. Come here!" he commanded. "Let's talk."

Angel, eyes wide with fear, yanked free of his grip and ran screaming toward the door.

"Can't nobody hear you!" Jordan snarled as he moved in front of the door and locked it. "It's just me and you." He grabbed her again, both arms this time, and dragged her, kicking and screaming, toward her bedroom.

"You can't do this!" she cried. "I'm only thirteen! I'm your daughter! How can you do this to me! NO! STOP!"

"You ain't my daughter," Jordan sneered as he tried to force her to the bed. "You skinny little weakling! Your mama had lots of boyfriends. You ain't none of mine!"

The months of exercise and dance practice had made Angel a lot stronger than

174

Jordan expected, but he still managed to have her under his power with little difficulty. Weeping and terrified, Angel begged him to leave her alone. When he touched her face, she screamed again. He slapped her. She shuddered with despair.

In the kitchen, the pot of hot dogs, which had long since boiled out of water, was seething and shaking on top of the wild gas flames. The meat, crisp and split, ignited into a small flame, which found new fuel in the spots of grease upon the stove. Soon the whole stove was covered with hot flames that licked and devoured everything they touched. The apartment had no smoke alarm, so Jordan never even noticed the smoke or the smell.

TWENTY-THREE

After the tournament, Gerald got off the bus feeling vaguely uneasy. He wished again that he could live someplace where graffiti didn't decorate every empty corner, where trees grew thick enough to get lost in. He glanced toward his building, standing tall and dark against the sky, puffs of thin gray smoke coming from an upstairs window.

Smoke? Gerald thought. He was running before he was even aware of it. As he rushed up the six flights of stairs, he remembered the taste of smoke in his mouth, the touch of the smoke-filled air in his nose and lungs, and the colors of the bright orange heat. He thought back to that long-ago day behind the couch of his mother's house — the fear, the flames, the sweet, silent peace of a final sleep — and then he thought of Angel. He knew that the smoke was coming from his apartment, he knew that Angel was up there, and he knew that Jordan was with her. He screamed. *"Angel!"*

He could hear the sirens faintly in the

distance, but his thoughts were only on Angel and the top of the stairs. When he reached the door, he pounded on it so hard his fists throbbed.

"Angel!" he shouted. *"Angel!"* He tried the other apartments on the floor, but the doors were either flung open or locked; everyone had either fled the fire or was out. Finding only silence and smoke, Gerald fumbled hastily for his key.

Please don't let me be too late! he silently prayed. *Where is Jordan?* he wondered as he dropped the key. *And where is Monique? Is Angel in there alone?*

Gerald found the key and turned the lock fiercely to the right. When the cool outside air from the hall rushed inside, the flames swelled and raged. Gerald panicked a moment as his memories of flames engulfed him. He wanted to run and hide behind a sofa and wait for Mama to come. . . .

Mama will be here soon — No — Mama is downstairs, high again, gone again, gone again. . . .

"NO!" he said fiercely as he thought of Angel. He glanced toward the kitchen, which the flames were consuming with glee, and headed across the living room toward Angel's bedroom. Flames flickered

around the edges of the floor. He knew he only had seconds. *Where is Jordan?* Gerald kept thinking.

He opened Angel's door, expecting to find her huddled under the bed or screaming at the window. Instead, what he saw made him forget the fire, forget the danger, forget the fears of the past. Angel lay on her bed, barely conscious. Jordan was walking slowly toward the foot of her bed. So intent was he that he didn't even notice Gerald.

"Don't you touch her, you perverted bastard!" Jordan spun around, amazed, and lunged toward Gerald with his fists.

"I shoulda killed you years ago," Jordan said with quiet ferocity. "You the one that sent me to jail. I ain't forgot that!" The room stank of Jordan's suffocating cologne, stifling smoke, and fear.

"Don't you know the house is on fire, fool?" Gerald said, stepping back two paces.

Jordan seemed to be suddenly aware of the heat, the smell of the flames, and the fire in Gerald's eyes. Ignoring them for the moment, he lunged toward Gerald again and knocked him to the ground. Gerald's head hit the edge of Monique's TV. He saw fire as the pain stunned him for a moment. He didn't even notice the blood from the cut at first.

The TV tottered for a moment, then plunged with a crash to the floor. The heavy iron television stand fell over seconds later, shattering the bedroom window. The cold air that rushed in gave Gerald the fresh breaths he needed, but it also fueled the anger of the flames in the apartment and in Jordan Sparks.

"That's the last time you're ever gonna touch me, or Angel!" Gerald swore through clenched teeth.

He jumped up and swung at Jordan fiercely, but missed. Gerald tried to dart out of the way of Jordan's kick, but he wasn't fast enough. With the steel toe of his cowboy boots, Jordan kicked Gerald squarely on his shin. Gerald screamed in pain. He heard the bone crack. He fell once again.

Angel, coughing and dizzy, struggled to sit up as the smoke began to come in through the open door.

Gerald glanced over at the helpless Angel, eased himself across the floor, and grabbed Jordan's leg. Jordan was stronger, but he was drunk and confused.

Gerald no longer felt fear or pain, only anger over the past — for Aunt Queen's

179

lost hugs and Angel's lost innocence, for Monique's dim weaknesses, Andy's unbearable guilt, and for Rob's fiery destruction. All of that was focused into his final lunge at Jordan. He reached for Jordan's leg and pulled hard.

Jordan stumbled, then fell with a crashing thud to the floor. Stunned only for a moment, he got up, glared at Gerald, saw the growing intensity of the fire, and moved toward the open door. He never even glanced back at Angel, who was conscious and crying.

Gerald struggled to stand as he heard Angel sobbing faintly. He pulled himself up to the bed. Angel, almost hysterical, was sucking in huge gulps of the smoke-filled air. As he reached her, she shuddered, and then lay still.

"Angel!" he yelled. Ignoring the pain in his leg and head, he covered her with a blanket and lifted her gently from the bed. She felt light in his arms — like a spirit, he thought as he shivered in spite of the heat. He could no longer see. He limped through the darkness and smoke, toward the open door.

The room began to spin as the darkness and the flames attacked Gerald. He wanted to hide behind the sofa. He wanted to let the flames take away all the pain forever, but he remembered Angel, and dragged himself toward the door, which seemed so far away. As he approached the doorway, he could no longer remember which way to go. Dark, thick smoke filled the top of the opening. Gerald coughed and stumbled. A large, hard object blocked the doorway. Gerald fell over it and rolled out of the door into the hall. In spite of his confusion and pain, he still managed to hang on to Angel. On the floor, he discovered the air was just a bit clearer. Gerald wiped his stinging eyes and saw that the stairs were smoky, but not yet on fire. Staying close to the floor, he snaked himself down the first flight of stairs, gently dragging the limp, unconscious body of Angel with him. He stopped at the landing, gasping and heaving, barely able to breathe the thin, clear air near the floor.

He heard thuds. He saw large black rubber boots. He heard voices.

"Hey! Get some oxygen up here! We found them!"

He heard clicks. He had heard that sound before . . . the click of a high heel shoe on a wooden step . . . going away . . . fading into the distance. But these clicks were close, then closer. They were hard and demanding and attached to a voice. Monique's.

"I told you my kids was in here! Hurry up!" she demanded shrilly. "Do something! I think they're dead! Where's Jordan?" Monique screamed hysterically.

"Ma'am, let us do our job. We told you not to follow. Max, get her out of here!"

Gerald grinned weakly just before he passed out. Monique. Just in time this time. Just in time.

TWENTY-FOUR

Angel's eyelids fluttered, then her eyes rolled in fear as she thrashed her arms wildly, pulling off the oxygen mask and screaming in terror. The paramedic held her arms gently and spoke softly. "It's gonna be okay. Relax. You swallowed quite a bit of smoke up there."

"Jordan! No! Fire!" she whispered incoherently. "Oh, Gerald, make it stop! Make it stop! Where's Gerald?" she asked with sudden fear.

"He's right here, right next to you. He saved your life, you know."

Angel relaxed when she saw him. Gerald, with large bandages on his head and his leg, and an oxygen mask on his face, grinned at her.

"You look like something out of a monster movie," she croaked. Her voice was raspy from the smoke. "What happened, Gerald?"

"I'm not sure," Gerald said slowly. "I remember carrying you, and falling, and . . . Monique. Monique's shoes on the

183

steps," he said, remembering.

Monique peeked her head into the back of the ambulance then. "How's my babies?"

"Ain't no babies here, Mama," Angel whispered with a weak smile. "I think we gonna be okay."

Gerald frowned. "Monique, where's Jordan? He left us there to die in the fire. He had Angel . . . He was trying to . . . to . . . He tried to kill me!"

Monique's smile faded.

The paramedic and a police officer looked into the back of the ambulance. "Do you feel up to talking, son?"

Gerald nodded. At the word "son" he thought of Rob's dad. He knew Mr. Washington was only a phone call away. That made him feel better — relaxed and safe.

"There was another man in the apartment," the police officer said. "Was he a relative?"

"He's no relation of mine!" growled Gerald with hatred in his voice. "His name is Jordan Sparks. He claims to be Angel's father, but he's mean and hateful and he's a child molester! There! I said it, Monique! He tried to molest Angel and he's —"

"He's dead," the police officer cut in.

"Dead?"

"He died trying to get out of the apartment."

Gerald thought back to the haze and confusion of the fire. He remembered stumbling and falling over something — or was it some*one*? "Where did you find him?"

"He was lying right by the door," the officer said. "We think he slipped — he had on new boots with slick soles —"

And steel toes, Gerald thought.

"— and he must have fallen trying to run out of the apartment."

"Running out on you," Monique admitted slowly.

"I think," Gerald said slowly, "that Jordan is the reason we're still alive. I fell over his body on the way out of the door. That put us on the floor, where the air was breathable, and let me find the steps."

"And let us find you," the firefighter added.

Monique began to weep. She wept not for Jordan, whose spark was finally snuffed out, but for all of the flames of pain and hatred he had caused.

"May I ride with them?" she asked the paramedic when she could speak again.

He nodded. "Maybe you should ask them," he added, pointing to Gerald and Angel.

Angel, whose face was covered with tears, held out her arms to her mother. Gerald, relieved that they were alive and Jordan was not, smiled and nodded.

As Monique climbed into the back of the ambulance, an orange ball of fur leaped in front of her.

"Tiger!" Angel smiled with relief. The cat snuggled close to her and glared at the paramedic, who just smiled and pretended not to see it. The sirens screamed as they rode to the hospital.

"How do you like the music I picked for our ride downtown?" Gerald teased Angel.

"It's fine for the movie soundtrack, but I couldn't dance to it." She smiled and drifted off to sleep.

With the flames and fear behind them, Gerald and Angel rode together to the music of the sirens which had decorated their past and would forge their future.

For readers who would like further information or who need help, the following numbers are provided as a place to start:

1-800-422-4453
National Child Abuse Hotline

1-800-799-7233
National Domestic Violence Hotline

DISCUSSION TOPICS FOR FORGED BY FIRE

1. The first chapter of *Forged by Fire* was originally written and published as a short story. What elements enable this chapter to stand alone as a complete story? What elements in the story become thematically developed concepts in the novel? What is the effect of seeing the events of Chapter One develop through the eyes of a child? How does this method of telling the story affect the reader's response?

2. At the end of Chapter One, what assumptions or predictions might be made about Gerald? His future? His mother? Would those predictions be the same if Chapter One is read only as a short story that ends with Gerald curled up behind the sofa and seeing "colors with his eyes closed?"

3. Discuss the use of music and color as images in the story that expand into

thematic ideas. How is music laced into the lives of Gerald and Angel, and how does music allow Angel moments of release from her pain? Show how the use of color, or the lack of it, clarifies the lives of Angel and Gerald.

4. Many young people live in homes where abuse is a secret, silent pain. Discuss how realistically the lives of Gerald and Angel are portrayed and how these characters can become a voice for young readers who are afraid to speak out.

5. Discuss the socioeconomic level at which Gerald's family lives. Discuss abuse as a family problem, not merely a problem of a certain level of society. How might the story have included a broader base of society to demonstrate that the problem of abuse is found at all social and economic levels?

6. How are Gerald and Angel like many young people today? How are they different? What strengths do they possess that help them survive the situation in which they live?

7. Describe the relationship between the friends in the book (Gerald and his friends, Gerald and Mr. Washington, Angel and Kiara). Is friendship enough when situations become overwhelming to young people?

8. Gerald's mother Monique had numerous problems. She loved him, but seemed to be consumed with her own troubles. Why was Monique not willing or able to see Jordan's abuse of Angel? How realistic do you think Monique's reaction is?

9. Monique is abused as well — physically and emotionally. What relationship do you think there is between domestic violence and child abuse? Why do you think this relationship exists?

10. How can families learn to cope effectively with tragedy, pain, and adversity? When is it necessary to seek assistance from someone outside the family?

11. Why did Angel let Jordan's abuse continue? Why didn't she tell

someone about it? What effect did Jordan's abuse have on Angel's life? What long-range consequences might result from such abuse?

12. What are some of the difficulties created by discussing the problem of physical and sexual abuse in a novel for young adults? What positive influences can result from talking about these problems?

13. Discuss the character of Jordan Sparks. Does he have any redeeming qualities, or is he purely a negative character? What might have made Jordan the person he is?

14. Discuss the character of Aunt Queen. What are her limitations? What are her strengths? How does the memory of Aunt Queen's strength affect and influence the rest of Gerald's life?

15. Describe the gradual buildup to the final confrontation between Jordan and Gerald. What makes this inevitable? How is fire an important image in the concluding action between them? Why is this significant? Could

the novel have been resolved without the death of Jordan? Explain.

16. What does Angel's love of ballet reflect about her life, her pain, and her personality? Why is dancing an easy way to explain complicated feelings? How can self-expression be used as a tool for helping or healing?

17. Explain the title of the novel. Define the word "forged." What references can be found to "fire?" How is fire an image of pain as well as release for Gerald and Angel? Why does the title have more than one possible interpretation?

ACTIVITIES
AND RESEARCH

1. You are a reporter at one of the following scenes. Write the story for your newspaper.
   — the fire at Gerald's apartment at the beginning of the book
   — the fire at Gerald's apartment at the end of the book

2. Investigate child abuse and/or domestic violence. Call the phone numbers at the back of the book and ask about the best place to go for written information. (Do not tie up their lines — they are for people in crisis.) Find out how you can best help in your community.

3. Investigate recent laws in your community concerning those who are convicted of child abuse or domestic violence. What is the usual punishment in your community? Is Jordan's punishment realistic or unrealistic?

What do you think should be the punishment for adults convicted of child abuse? Call your local library. They can direct you to sources that can easily summarize this information for you.

4. Create a conversation between Aunt Queen and Gerald, or Aunt Queen and Angel. What would she say to them during the worst of their problems with Jordan and Monique? At the end of the book?

5. Write a letter to one of the characters in the book explaining your feelings about the events in the story. What advice would you give either Angel, Gerald, Monique, or Jordan?

ABOUT THE AUTHOR

SHARON M. DRAPER has been writing and teaching for more than twenty years. Her first novel, *Tears of a Tiger*, received the first Coretta Scott King Genesis Award. Currently chair of the English department at Walnut Hills High School in Cincinnati, she was recently honored as the 1997 National Teacher of the Year. She lives in Cincinnati, Ohio.